Evvy's
Civil War

Evvy's
Civil War

Miriam Brenaman

G. P. Putnam's Sons
New York

Library of Congress Cataloging-in-Publication Data
Brenaman, Miriam. Evvy's civil war / by Miriam Brenaman.
p. cm. Summary: In Virginia in 1860, on the verge of the Civil War,
fourteen-year-old Evvy chafes at the restrictions that her
society places on both women and slaves.
[1. Sex role—Fiction. 2. Slavery—Fiction.
3. Underground railroad—Fiction. 4. African Americans—Fiction.
5. Virginia—History—Civil War, 1861–1865—Fiction.
6. United States—History—Civil War, 1861–1865—Fiction.] I. Title.
PZ7.B7504 Lad 2002   [Fic]—dc21   2001018353
ISBN 0-399-23713-5
1 3 5 7 9 10 8 6 4 2
First Impression

This book is dedicated to the memory of the women who survived the Civil War and in its aftermath created new opportunities for the generations of girls following them. To three of those women, I make a special dedication:

Frances Taylor Boykin, "Fanny"
My great-grandmother

Virginia Randolph Ellett, "Miss Jenny"
Founder of my preparatory school

Martha Carey Thomas, "Minnie" who became "Carey"
Guiding light of my college, Bryn Mawr

Acknowledgments

My thanks, first, to my editor, Victoria Wells, whose enthusiasm for this story survived the long and tedious process needed to guide it from first draft to completed book. Then, thanks to all my readers: to Audrey Couloumbis, who read the chapters in patches and batches as I finished them, and made coherent suggestions; to Barbara, who read the first chapter at the copier and encouraged me by frequently asking for more; to Olivia, Melissa, Jennifer, and Clarese, my young readers who took to the role of test-market with gusto. More gratitude goes to Charlotte Sheedy, my agent, and her associate Jonathan, who relieved me of the business aspects of publishing. And a special thanks to my husband, Bob Cretsinger, for his economic and emotional support while I wrote.

Table of Contents

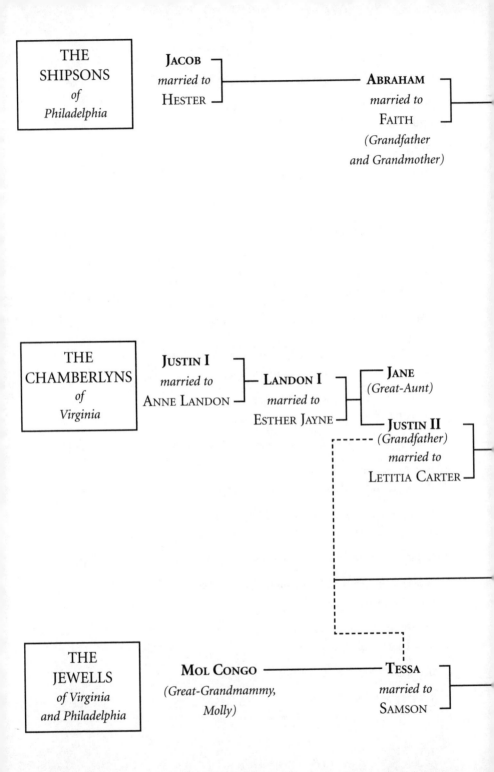

THE
SHIPSONS
of
Philadelphia

JACOB
married to
HESTER

ABRAHAM
married to
FAITH
*(Grandfather
and Grandmother)*

THE
CHAMBERLYNS
of
Virginia

JUSTIN I
married to
ANNE LANDON

LANDON I
married to
ESTHER JAYNE

JANE
(Great-Aunt)

JUSTIN II
(Grandfather)
married to
LETITIA CARTER

THE
JEWELLS
*of Virginia
and Philadelphia*

MOL CONGO
*(Great-Grandmammy,
Molly)*

TESSA
married to
SAMSON

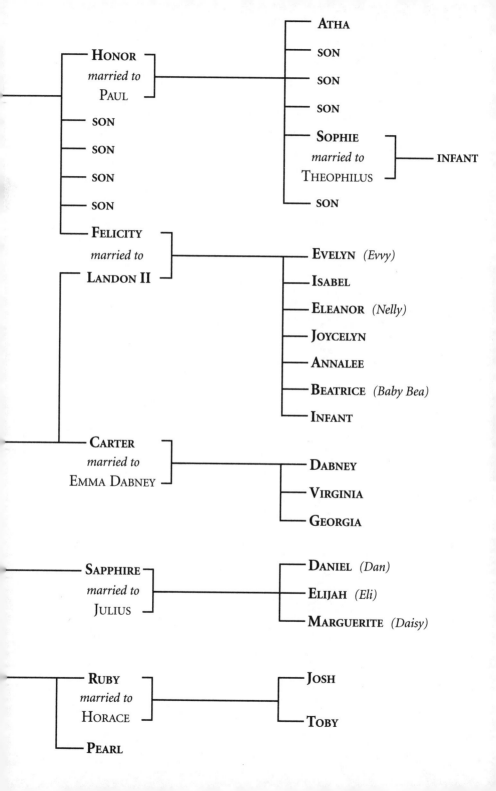

Prologue

In Which I Introduce Myself
and Wax Philosophical

WHEN I was twelve, three years before the war, Papa caught me eavesdropping outside his bedroom.

Mama was again wearing the Chinese jacket that foretold another baby, but even Sapphire refused to discuss how or why my parents kept making this mistake. I had hoped to find out for myself the reason behind this endless series of younger sisters.

Papa confined me to the guest-room bed for three days to reflect on the sinfulness of eavesdropping, with only a Bible to read. Though I appreciated a bed and room to myself, after a few hours I did regret the solitude.

The most lasting result of that punishment was that I discovered the Good Book was full of stories our minister never discussed from the pulpit, and I took to reading it regularly. Papa rejoiced to see me on the *upward path;* we were both happy.

Sapphire brought my meals and took away the chamber pot, which surely was a nuisance for her, in addition to all her other work. If she'd given me what-for, I couldn't have blamed her.

Yet all she said was, "Honey, your papa's a good man. Trouble is, he's never been a woman or a slave, so he can't understand. There're times you've got to know things, no matter how you find them out. Times you got to do something, even if it's wrong." She was right. She usually was.

My friend Liza Wright, always indifferent to sin, disagreed. "My mama says Virginia gentlemen don't like clever women; a girl should be ignorant and act more ignorant than she is. Especially when she's only passable in looks."

"But, Liza, Mama's clever, and Papa adores her."

She shrugged. "Your mama's a Beauty. Beauties get away with anything. Even brains. Or no dowry." She slid me a sideways look. She, too, was only passable. But very rich.

I pondered all this, and still figured eavesdropping was necessary, especially for the merely passable. Getting caught was the problem. I would not get caught again.

There is simply something wrong with my conscience. I do try to wrestle with the devil as I ought, but, like Eve, when tempted by the Forbidden Fruit of the Tree of Knowledge, I succumb. Good as they are, how could my parents have bred a daughter like me?

Sapphire once said to me, "Child, I wish your grandpappy Marse Justin and his sister, your great-aunt Jane, had lived long enough for you to know them. You favor them awful much."

"Awful" may be the right word, though Sapphire was laughing. I feel better when somebody sensible like Sapphire—somebody who knows the real me—finds me amusing and practical instead of deep-dyed in sin.

One

In Which I Become a Lady Against My Will

UNTIL my fourteenth birthday I never pondered over my life, largely because it suited me. I took the good as normal and complained of the bad.

I was not pleased, for instance, to have five younger sisters, but at least I was the oldest. I got to boss the others and to go with Mama to visit her sister and my cousins in Philadelphia.

I was also to inherit Great-aunt Jane's gold locket, though all the rest of her jewelry had been left to Uncle Carter and would go to his girls. That infuriated my next-younger sisters Isabel and Nelly, as well as my Richmond cousins—but seemed fine to me.

As eldest, I also got the separate bedroom when Baby Beatrice (the latest in the line of baby sisters that the Chinese jacket had foretold) became old enough to move from the crib to the trundle. This sent Annalee to half of Joycelyn's double bed, so Nelly was bumped to share with Isabel. No more kicking and bedclothes snatching for me. Good-bye, nursery!

I was quite set up in my own space, in Great-aunt Jane's big four-poster with the embroidered hangings, her writing desk (purchased in Paris during Jane's Grand Tour), and a window seat perfect for reading undisturbed. It was old-fashioned stuff, of course, not like the modern carved mahogany furniture in the school mansion, but it suited me.

I was not nice about sharing, but, if Joycelyn begged very hard, I let her read there, too. She was like me, dark-haired and brown-eyed, and boisterous when she wasn't reading. I played mad when she tagged after me and Sapphire's daughter, Daisy, but, secretly, I wished she were next in age instead of fourth down, after Isabel and Nelly.

Somehow, I had managed to ignore the inescapable and fast-approaching martyrdom of becoming a lady. I knew, of course, that fourteen was the age my parents had appointed, but I hadn't expected to plunge in all at once.

On the birthday morn, Mama and Sapphire and the girls poured giggling into my chamber, bearing in high good humor the most horrible gifts.

"Good morning, Darling," Mama greeted me, holding Baby in one arm, while waving a *corset*, of all things, in the other.

"Look, Evelyn, look at this!" Isabel held a rose-colored silk-and-lace gown against her body, to display its charms before draping it reverently over the back of my chair. It clung without wrinkling; yards of skirt billowed over the arms and seat. "We picked pink to go with your coloring," she added. Blonde as she was, she'd expect blue when her turn came, two years from now.

"I helped," announced Nelly, pointing to embroidery. "See that? Mama wouldn't let Joycelyn do any, 'cause she's still on her sampler. But I did all that. No blood-pricks, either."

For a moment her smug satisfaction made my hand itch to swat her, but Mama's face was alight with pleasure, so I merely muttered, "My. Lovely," and bared my teeth in Nelly's direction. She'd annoyed me from birth, and in ten years she'd not improved.

Or maybe I hadn't. "Blackgum and Thunder," Sapphire calls us. By which she means we're equally troublesome. Well, we do both nose out secrets, but I don't tell. Nelly couldn't keep a secret if you gave it to her in a locked trunk.

"Look!" yelled Joycelyn, stamping in her eagerness to be noticed. She popped a crinoline from semihiding behind her back. The thing bounced merrily in the air, its hoops incredibly wide. Frightening.

"Me, too!" Little Annalee ran forward, clutching a handful of large tortoiseshell hairpins. "See what I've got."

I looked to Sapphire for help, but she merely took Baby Beatrice from Mama and smiled. "Gonna look mighty grown up, Miss Evelyn." She'd never called me "Miss Evelyn" before.

They converged upon me, stripping off the nightgown after I put my smallclothes beneath, and Mama clasped the corset around me, ordering, "Now hold on to the bedpost, Evvy, while I lace this. We won't do it tight to start."

Well! It felt mighty tight to me. And where I'd begun to get a little bigger up top, suddenly I had a bosom. Really. All the extra flesh got pushed up. I looked down on two little—well, not even so very little—humps poking above my camisole.

"Look at Evvy!" said Annalee, pointing with a hand full of hairpins. "Mama, look."

Mama blushed a bit, and patted my cheek, but said to Annalee, "Don't point, Dearest, it's rude. And we don't speak of ladies' figures in public."

"This ain't public," said Annalee, with perfect four-year-old honesty, "and Evvy ain't a lady, either."

"Not 'ain't,' Annalee. You know better than that."

"Here, let me now." Joycelyn gestured with the crinoline. "Bend down, Evvy, so's I can slip it over." She straightened the thing around my hips, then tried to hook the waistband. Mercy! My waist was *still* too large. *"Ummph."* With a great yank, she pulled the band tight and fastened it.

At eight, she had six years of freedom before this could happen to her. I felt my gorge rise in my throat, perhaps with envy, perhaps with the pressure on my stomach. Suddenly, Joycelyn was shy. "I'll miss you, Evvy," she whispered.

It came to me that I'd never climb a fence or ford a stream or swing a rope from the hayloft again, not in all my life.

Joycelyn would tag after someone else now. Ruby's boys, maybe, but not Sapphire's daughter, Daisy. She'd be fourteen, too, in just three days. Something would happen to her, I figured, though she'd not be expected to be a "lady."

"Now, Evvy, thee will have to sit, so's I can do up thy hair," Mama said. I knew she was excited, or she'd never have slipped and "Thou'd" me. She was raised Quaker, but when she married Papa and came to Virginia she put that behind. Mostly, anyway. Since our recent trip to Philadelphia to visit her mama and sister, the habit came back sometimes.

"Isabel, thee and Nelly move that dress so Evvy can sit, but mind thee doesn't wrinkle it."

The girls pounced on the dress, one to a side, and swooped it from the chair. Mama advanced, brush in hand, to tame my thick dark hair, still tangled from the pillow.

"Pull the hoop up in back before you sit," she suggested. Too late. The blamed thing ballooned in front, giving my sisters a good look at my underpinnings and a case of the titters. I tried again, and the hoop subsided.

Mama twisted a corkscrew of hair in back, and began to anchor the mass with a score of hairpins, handed over by Annalee. They scratched.

"Oh, Evvy, you look a grown lady, after all!" said Annalee.

"Here." Isabel thrust the dress at Nelly. "Hand this to me when I'm settled." She leapt onto the high bed. The ropes under the mattress groaned with her weight, then groaned again as Nelly scrambled up. I groaned, too, as I rose from the chair.

"Never you mind, Miss Evvy," Sapphire's voice reassured from behind. "You'll get the hang of it soon."

My sisters stood on the bed's edge, the rose-silk gown triumphantly aloft between them. "Come here, Evvy; we'll drop this over without mussing your hairdo," said Nelly.

I stood, and tried to nod, but the Edifice that was now my hair threatened to tumble. I'd have to walk as we'd practiced, with books on our heads. Perfect posture from now on.

I put a tentative foot forward, then another, as the crinoline bumped and swayed around me.

I turned and backed to the bed, and the silk whispered over my head and arms, slithering as it went. Wadded things in the armpit made the sleeves oddly tight. A scent of attar of roses wafted from them.

"Can we take these out?" I asked Mama. "I can't move my arms much, and I'm not even hooked up yet."

"Oh, no, Darling. Those pads keep the dress fresh, especially in this late summer heat. We can't wash silk, you know." Mama blushed a bit. "Now that you're grown, you'll need to protect against staining. And . . . well, odor. Besides, in a good dress, you mustn't use your arms much, or you'll tear the seams."

Mama began hooking the cleverly hidden plackets together, and the bodice tightened, alarmingly low over my newly created bosom.

I could never drop or spill again. Or perspire.

No. It couldn't be this bad all the time. My own mother had

dresses of washable cotton or practical tarlatan, and did arm-using jobs around the plantation every day. I could see no outline of sweat pads in her sleeves this morning. But her skirts were also a foot-tangling length, and her hair was anchored with hairpins.

I had never considered that her blonde curls might be uncomfortable. They looked so becoming, with a few tendrils escaping around her forehead and in front of her ears. Most of my sisters were blonde, and some might turn out as charmingly as Mama, but I had small hope for myself or Joycelyn. We had the dark Chamberlyn looks.

Little Annalee began patting the yards of rosy folds into place. "It smells good!" She buried her face in the fabric.

Joycelyn jerked her away. "Don't wipe your nose in it, Silly."

"Mama, I want one, too!" said Annalee.

"Not yet," Mama said. "All in good time." She swept Annalee toward her in a hug. "I'm cutting down Joycelyn's white dimity for you. Very suitable and pretty. You may have a new sash, if you want."

"A blue silk ribbon one?" asked Annalee. "Real long?"

"Long and wide, too." Mama smiled at all of us. "Next visit to Uncle Carter and Aunt Emma in Richmond, we'll shop for fresh sashes and bonnet trims for everyone." A cheer arose, which I could not join.

"Now, we must show you off to Papa!" Isabel said. She and Nelly raced to the head of the stairs and began to bump each other on the way down, Joycelyn and Annalee close behind.

"Papa, Papa, come to the hall and see!" yelled Nelly.

I groped my way to the head of the stairs, sliding one foot before the other. A glance down told me I couldn't see my feet, or the stair treads, either.

"Hold the railing, Miss Evelyn," Sapphire's voice urged. "You'll get the feel of it soon."

The stairs curved down before me; my dress billowed over the edge, swaying against both wall and balustrade. I slipped a toe over the brink, then slid it forward to the next tread. Then the other foot. The silk made a slushing sound, and there was a soft *whap* as the bottom ring of the hoop hit wood.

Below, Papa and my sisters stood, foreshortened and small, their faces turned up to watch my descent.

Hair high, head aching, stomach churning, bosoms bouncing, I walked down the stairs to face ladyhood.

Two

In Which I Acquire My Locket
and Am Ordered
to Attend a Dinner

BREAKFAST started well enough, with the presentation of Great-aunt Jane's gold locket, which I'd never worn before.

Papa clasped it around my neck. The golden oval nestled into my new bosom, and I viewed the large central diamond with delight.

Set into the inside were miniature portraits on ivory of Grandfather Justin and his twin sister, Jane, at about my own age. Their clever, sharp-looking features were oddly identical under the old-fashioned hairstyles of their day. Only the brilliant blue of Justin's eyes differed from his dark-eyed sister—and from me.

"You will have to work hard to deserve this lady's legacy," Papa said. As always, his voice was reverent as he recalled the woman who'd raised him. "She sacrificed her own happiness to make a home for her brother and his two little boys," he continued. "Brother Carter and I can never be too grateful."

I'd heard of the virtuous Jane all my childhood—how, though spirited, popular, and wealthy, she'd refused all offers of marriage to raise her nephews. I doubted I'd live up to her inner beauty. Yet, I at least looked like her on the outside—a favorable bit of luck that had caused her to leave me this gem.

I was, by family consensus, Jane's spit image. Even Joycelyn's features were softer. Little Beatrice had inherited Justin's brilliant eyes—but my mother's beauty. "Going to be a *man trap* someday, that baby, sure as shooting," Sapphire's sister Ruby predicted.

"You may wear this for occasions," Papa said, "but your mother's to keep it safely in her jewel casket until you marry."

"If she doesn't marry, Papa, can I have it?" asked Isabel. "I'm next oldest."

"That's not fair!" exclaimed Nelly. "Aunt Jane gave it *specifically* to Evelyn 'cause she was already born, but you weren't born, any more than I was, before she died. So, whether you're next or not doesn't matter."

"Girls!" said Mama. "No arguing. There's no reason to think Evvy won't marry."

"Maybe she'll die," suggested Annalee, quite without malice. "Then she couldn't get married, could she?"

"Well, if she *died,* she wouldn't need the locket, Silly," Joycelyn said. "Besides, Aunt Jane gave it to Evvy because she looked like her. I look like Evvy, so I get it if she doesn't."

"Daughters! Any more of this talk, and you'll go without breakfast," said Papa. "Fair or not, the necklace is Evelyn's. Please sit." He pulled out Mama's chair for her.

"Well, it's unjust," Nelly mumbled. "Cousin Georgia and Cousin Virginia get all the other jewelry, and we don't get anything."

"Nelly, perhaps your cousins would complain it was unjust for me to inherit your grandfather's estate, while their own father, only a year younger after all, got Aunt Jane's. That, however, was their decision, and a Will is a sacred thing."

"And very lucky we all are, too," Mama said. "Your aunt

Emma would pine and perish in the country, and Georgia and Virginia suffer vastly from *ennui* when they visit. Even young Dabney bides country life poorly, once he's had his fill of hunting. Aunt Jane's Richmond house suits them perfectly."

"What's *on-we?*" Annalee whispered, tugging my dress.

"French for boredom; don't interrupt," I whispered back.

Mama gave the dimpled smile I so admired. It hinted at the frivolous side we only saw occasionally.

"Your uncle thrives in a city law practice, while the plantation is the perfect place for your papa's Academy." She smiled again. "And *I* might pine away in the city. So, let us give thanks to our Lord for the blessings of this table *and* for the sensible division devised by thy granddaddy and his sister."

With this, we sat; our father said grace, and we began to consume the breakfast served by Sapphire and Daisy, my playmate and friend. Daisy raised her brow and opened her eyes wide, to acknowledge my transformation. We'd talk later.

For a while my sisters and I were almost silent. It was rare for Papa to breakfast with us. He usually went across the park to eat, to keep the boys of Chamberlyn Academy mannerly. He deplored biscuit fights and such disruptions. I was flattered that he'd joined us for my birthday, and not surprised when he cleared his throat—his usual signal for pronouncements.

"Evelyn, you've turned fourteen on a fortuitous day. You'll be able to try your wings in several ways."

"What do you mean, Papa?" I was distracted for fear a drop of soft-boiled egg or a squirt of sausage might hit the rose silk. I had tucked my napkin into the neckline of the new dress, but Mama had removed it and settled it in my lap.

How to eat enough, with my waist so tight? How to keep from splitting the seams?

"We have a speaker scheduled today for the students," Papa began. "An English clergyman touring our country. Bernard Smithson of Madisonville Academy particularly recommended him, and I gather he's very well regarded. I was fortunate to get him. I'll be off to the depot to pick him up after breakfast."

"Do you know his topic, Dearest?" asked Mama.

"Why, no. Bernard said his speech was entirely suitable for Southern Gentlemen's sons, and would enhance any institution's reputation."

Papa paused, wiped his mouth, and then announced the real treat. "Of course, we plan the usual formal dinner with faculty tonight to honor him. Evvy can wear this lovely new dress, and help Mama hostess. It will be a grand opportunity."

"But, Papa!" I could barely stand breakfast in this outfit. How was I to accomplish dinner? Or an afternoon of sitting, bored by a long-winded preacher? One sermon, on Sunday, was more than enough. "None of the other girls has to. It's not fair!"

"I am tired of hearing what's not fair!" Papa crumpled his napkin. "Never use that phrase again, any of you!"

He turned to me. "You are eldest, Evelyn. You must set an example. You have your own room, the locket, a new dress, *and* the responsibilities that attach to growing up."

He frowned around the table. "As for the rest of you girls, you have your share, too, or will in time."

Here, Mama intervened. "Indeed, your papa provides all you need and asks little but dutiful respect in return." We girls looked at her, startled. We were used to Papa's frequent demands for improvement, but any rebuke from Mama was noteworthy.

Suddenly she relented, and smiled, using the drawl she affected when she pretended to have been raised a Southern Belle. "You-all would shorely suffah if your papah's Academy weren't so distractin'. Why, he haa-dly has time fo' noticin' yoah excessive vanities. As fo' little me, as a citified girl, I would be toh-tally dee-strowid with gossipin' and pah-ty goin'. Ah shorely would *not* hev time for tutorin' a passel of rapscallions such as yo'sefs." She fluttered her eyelashes, sending us into a fit of the giggles, saving breakfast from disaster.

Three

In Which I First Glimpse
the Enemy

THE property as Grandpapa Justin had left it to Papa had two large residences on it, some outbuildings, the surrounding park, and not much else. Acreage and fieldhands had been sold off to pay the debts of the estate before Papa inherited what was left.

The older house was the graceful Georgian building where my family lived. This was called the Big House, though it was far smaller than the Tudor-style mansion that held the Academy.

Old Justin and Jane had spent at least one of their fortunes erecting that edifice to live in themselves, when they made a gift of the original house to my parents at their marriage. The barn was now a gymnasium for the Academy, but the stable still held our carriage horses and a few mounts owned by wealthy boarding students.

On either side of our own home were smaller brick buildings, forming a U shape with the Big House. One, once the plantation office, was now used by Mama for business management of the school; the other was originally the kitchen, before the new kitchen with improvements, such as the iron stove and the washbasin that drained to the yard, had been attached to the house.

Behind the kitchen were a garden and the quarters. Like the Big House, these small slave cabins were built of brick fired from the red clay of the plantation. Most were empty, and, like the old kitchen, were boarded up for safety.

The Big House, kitchen, office, and quarters were half the park's length away from the other, more elaborate cluster of buildings surrounding the Tudor mansion. An easy walk for Papa, but distant enough for privacy. A small forest of huge oak trees and a knob of a hill hid each group of buildings from the other.

I never understood why Papa's father and aunt fancied the mansion as a home, but it made an excellent school. The downstairs held the classrooms and reception areas and also a ballroom now used as the refectory. It was emptied of tables once a year to become a dancing floor again. Upstairs were dormitories for boarding students and small apartments for masters. The oak-carved library was the Chapel and Lecture Hall.

So it was, that afternoon, that I found myself squirming on a bench next to Mama, in the Chapel, wearing my old yellow Sunday dress with hem let down, waist pinched in. To avoid thoughts of physical discomfort, dinner, and the lecture, I examined the stained-glass windows installed by my grandfather.

I peered under my bonnet brim at the room. I'd seldom seen it, as the Academy was forbidden territory for us girls. Suddenly, realization hit me: Unlike our church's windows, which depicted apostles, angels, and sheep, these windows depicted famous lovers. Juliet bent to a vine-climbing Romeo; Heloise kissed Abelard over a scroll; Cleopatra—heavens to Betsy!—had *naked bosoms* below her Egyptian necklace, glowing through a haze of after-added, sun-faded paint.

My hand flew to my mouth to stop the giggle bubbling up.

New ideas about old Justin's personality tickled my mind. No one had ever *hinted* his taste might run in this fashion. Of course, I might ask Sapphire. . . .

A boy across the aisle cleared his throat, and I jerked my head down. A sideways glance confirmed the worst. He'd caught me inspecting Cleopatra's bosom.

He grinned. Oh, no! Liza's older brother, Win, actually Winston Wright IV. A day student. *Worse and worse,* I thought. Win had ignored me ever since he'd been a lordly seven-year-old, buddying up with my visiting cousin Dabney and calling four-year-old Liza and me "stupid girls" and "babies." I felt my face burn with embarrassment, but the giggle shook me again.

There was no help for it. I must attend to the lecture—or sermon, for that was what it seemed to be. Boredom was my best hope for ladylike behavior.

Unfortunately, the man now stopped droning Bible passages and started interpreting them. To his mind, slavery was sanctioned by mention in the Sacred Book. "Shall we break faith with Abraham, Moses, and the Prophets?" he thundered from the podium. He then informed us of the duty of White men to rule, the duty of slaves to obey, and the duty of the Church to avoid politics.

I felt Mama sit up straighter, and a glance showed she wore what I thought of as her "Quaker face." She and Papa avoided speaking of slavery in my hearing, but I'd heard her express her dislike of "the peculiar institution" in conversations with her relatives in Philadelphia.

It was, however, the speaker's next argument that gripped my attention, as he discoursed on female duties.

"Those that hold slavery to be unjust wish to pervert the

marriage relationship as well," he proclaimed. "Woman has the obligation to obey. A husband, Lord and Master, nature has designed for every woman."

I was *not* inclined to think any pimply-faced boy could one day be Lord and Master over me! Yet, the words rolling off his tongue, poisoning the air and those boys' minds, held me in horrid fascination. Nobody else looked disturbed. Not even Papa, facing me on the podium, or Mama, who'd relaxed after the speaker stopped claiming the Bible supported slavery.

"Young men," he exhorted the students, "do not fail to use this precious time to prepare for the futures that await you. Each must fit himself, first and foremost, to rule as *paterfamilias* of a home. Some may seek a larger sphere as well—law, government, even a religious calling. Prepare now!"

He moderated his voice to add, almost carelessly, "Of course, one primary duty must be to see your sons educated to replace you, and to severely limit education for the slaves and daughters God may see fit to place in your care." He leaned forward to emphasize his next point.

"I earnestly urge you, for your domestic comfort, to seek unlettered wives. For," he said, "education improves the White man, but the Female, like the Savage, is weakened thereby. Science pronounces that the woman who studies is lost."

He further explained that Latin and algebra shriveled a woman's womb, so she produced sickly infants—or none at all. "You young men would have to go to Europe to find suitable brides.

"She must never read novels, which are corrupting to the already morally weak. *But,* far worse is exposure to philosophy, science, or mathematics."

He then leaned over the lectern to deliver his strongest

argument. *"The educated woman has sinfully used up in her own life all that was meant for her descendants.*

"A woman, in short, has but one duty: To obey her husband. And but one consolation: The sweet privileges of wife and mother. Any other enjoyment is *sinful.*"

Well, as much as I admired Mama, I'd never thought her wifely and motherly duties were "sweet." Arduous was more like it. And her scholarship hadn't prevented babies one whit. Healthy ones, too. Couldn't it be that babies, not books, might sap a woman's strength?

Nobody, I thought, *could call Mama sinful. And, just what is an* un*married female to do? Fold her hands and do nothing while waiting for an eligible offer?*

Could it be that virtuous ladyhood demanded a lifetime of boredom?

In Which I Fire
My First Shots

I ESCAPED across the park, leaving Mama to socialize, and ran to the kitchen, ready to pounce when she entered.

Sapphire's sisters, Ruby and Pearl, and Ruby's young sons, Josh and Toby, were fixing for the dinner I was set on avoiding. Ruby clanged burners on the newfangled stove, and Pearl had lumps of dough rising under clean washrags on the table nearest the stove's warmth.

The boys supposedly were helping but mostly were throwing potato peels into the hogwash, cackling whenever the other one missed the bucket.

Baby Beatrice chirped from her corner. She was still swaddled in long skirts and often damp, but already expert at enticing attention. Annalee, though, was tired and cross; she wandered whining, grabbing Mama's skirt as she entered.

Perhaps this was not the best moment to plead against attending dinner, but I plunged ahead. "Mama, I can't sit through dinner with that man! It's not fair. Papa won't let me talk, and there'll be nobody but boring old faculty—Professor Newland and Mr. Rawley's simpering wife. Oh, do talk Papa out of it!"

Mama slipped an apron over her good gown and stuck a

hand in the oven. Calm as always, she spoke to Ruby first. "This is not quite hot enough, Ruby. Two more sticks should do it."

She turned to me, and said, "It so happens, Dearest, I agree with your father that you'll benefit from mingling in society."

She hugged me lightly. "I want my daughters to learn before they are obliged to entertain. An occasional dinner at my own table while you're still young enough to be seen and not heard is a way to start."

She put a gentle finger on my lips. "No, no more. Go sponge off and change into the new rose dress. You may wear the locket tonight. And perhaps you'll find adults are not boring."

———

THE dining room, though worn, looked impressive. I glanced around, enjoying the room with candles lit and silver in use.

Tonight, we even had a butler. Ruby's husband, Horace, stood by Sapphire at the buffet. A free Negro, he hired himself out. Usually he worked for Papa, since he lived on our plantation with his wife and sons.

He was walking north from Georgia when he met Ruby, and he decided to stay. By law, ex-slaves had to move away from their homes when freed. This, Papa said, was because they might foment rebellion. Though why a stranger wouldn't foment just as well I couldn't say. Anyway, Horace did no fomenting. We were lucky he came.

The Honored Guest escorted Mama to her place, bowing to right and left and scattering compliments as he went. Mama complimented back, glowing in the candlelight that hid the exhaustion I'd begun to notice.

My parents had wedged me among my least-favorite people, where I'd resist any temptation to talk.

To my right was Professor Newland. Old Nincompoop to

me. Papa respected his mathematical ability. His silent wife sat across.

To my left, and overdressed as usual, was silly Mrs. Clayton Rawley, who never wore one ruffle where twenty could be crowded into use. Her handsome husband was Master of Latin and History, a former boxing champion at the College of William and Mary and, according to Papa, popular with the students.

The English visitor had barely tasted food when he stirred up trouble. "My dear Mr. Chamberlyn, what chance of election has this Mr. Lincoln, come November?"

"Not much," Papa replied, "given that he lacks polish, is married to a harridan, and my Northern correspondents write that no one there wants to endanger the Union. They know the South won't tolerate the man. Bell seems the better choice."

Mama disapproved of politics at the table. "Can I interest you in more relish? Our Ruby makes a fine one."

It was no use. The men argued on.

I was bored. Papa, Uncle Carter, and our neighbor Winston Wright III, father of Win and Liza, had already argued the subject to death.

Mrs. Rawley was bored, too. I watched her wiggle and lean forward, fingering her pearl necklace to distract the menfolk. I practiced being better behaved than a grown, married lady. The men took no notice of her, anyway. Something to consider.

Papa trotted out his usual arguments: "Why, our grand-fathers fought the Revolution together. My family has always attended Northern universities; many Southerners still do. My own wife has Pennsylvania relatives. Such ties are common-place." He finished with a flourish: "I tell you, Sir, we'll stay a Union! This is merely argument among family."

Mr. Rawley disagreed. "In my opinion, Sir, the South may *secede* if Lincoln wins, but there won't be *war*. The North don't like us; stands to reason they'll be happy to be shut of us. They've no stomach for a fight."

Old Newland now added his two cents' worth. "Those Yankees are moneygrubbing cowards. Not warriors." He nodded, setting several chins a-wobble. "Even our ladies have more courage," he added. "Why, I suspect they'd become Joans of Arc, should battle start!"

Mrs. Rawley seized this opening. "Oh, my dear Professor Newland! Not Southern ladies!"

And at this, the Reverend began again on "the sacred shrine of womanhood." My boredom ceased. I began to simmer.

I speared the last pickled peach from the cut-crystal server without dripping. I cut it into very small bites, so as not to feel queasy. My corset seemed to tighten as my irritation increased.

I tried to block the Englishman's voice, and I smiled demurely at my plate, picking each bite of peach separately.

To my horror, there was silence, and, ringing in my ears, a phrase addressing me. It had to be me, as I was the only "budding flower of womanhood" around.

"Sir?" I said. My stomach lurched as I glanced up.

"Do you not agree, Miss Evelyn, that a female is never justified in forsaking the sweet duties of wife and mother to pursue selfish talents?" His teeth gleamed above the blackness of his beard.

I couldn't refuse to speak. To agree was impossible. To disagree on my own say-so would be pert. My mind raced for an answer, from a respectable source.

The squirrel scampering in my brain suddenly squeaked

Bible. I'd taken to discussing oddments from The Book with Sapphire and Daisy. Parts the ministers skipped. Who could be more expert on virtue than Jesus?

I admit it, I smirked. What fun to smite the enemy with impeccable behavior! I laid the peach-picking fork down gently.

"Why, Sir, I believe our Lord's parable says talents are given to be used, and it's sinful to hide one's light under a bushel. Surely that applies to everyone? Even females?"

The group, doubtless mildly astonished, stared in silence. Emboldened, I seized one of Sapphire's favorite Bible stories.

"Why, Jesus even rebuked Martha when she ordered Mary to stop learning with the apostles, to serve in the kitchen. He said, 'Mary has chosen the better portion, which shall not be taken from her.' "

I glanced at Mama. Her eyebrows lifted; her mouth quirked in amusement, not shock.

The Englishman huffed, attracting all eyes. "Miss Evelyn, you must know '*The Devil can quote Scripture for his own purposes.*' Females must not interpret the Bible." His mouth was pursed in a pink bow of indignation; he waggled a finger at me.

"You were at my lecture today, Young Lady. Do you wish to *sin* by selfishly using for your own pleasure what was meant for your children and your children's children?"

I was genuinely puzzled. "But, Sir, how could females hurt children by learning? Mama's education *helps* us. Indeed, the whole neighborhood of girls would be ignorant if she'd hidden her talents under a bushel."

The Englishman glared, but said in a soothing voice, "Your papa gave me a tour of the property today, and I saw the girls' class set up in your Morning Room. I told him then—advanced instruction is hurtful to females, whether teacher or student."

He turned to my father and added, "In fact, my dear Chamberlyn, I should discourage your lovely wife from Latin, philosophy, and rhetoric, and higher mathematics as well."

Professor Newland agreed. His chins wobbled in passionate conviction: "There's no good side to that, neither. Latin don't make a woman more entertaining to her husband."

Mr. Rawley glanced away from his wife and said, "For myself, I believe an educated woman might add to a husband's enjoyment."

Papa was more definite. "Why, Sir, I could hardly have succeeded in my Academy without my wife's abilities." He bowed in Mama's direction. "Mrs. Chamberlyn has kept the books, managed the staff, and even taught the younger boys at times."

Having seized the floor, Papa continued: "England can, perhaps, afford merely decorative ladies." He smiled. "Our nation is less than a hundred years, however, and we need accomplished women to raise our citizens. I've encouraged my wife to teach girls, believing they will be improved as wives and mothers."

I should have had the sense to keep quiet.

"Why, you all—even Papa—believe the whole aim of a woman's life is to attain the blissful state of matrimony, and then—if she can manage it—bear children."

Neither the Newlands nor the Rawleys had offspring: I flushed with regret; it was too late to recall my words. I glanced from face to face, but none reassured.

The Reverend made a *tsk*ing sound, and said, "In marriage, Miss Evvy, husband and wife become One, and that One is the husband. That is indisputable. Surely you know it."

I pushed back, and stood. I had not been excused, but I knew I must leave, now, before I embarrassed my parents further.

"Quite so, Young Lady," said old Newland, glaring. His sad little wife whimpered and put her fingers to her mouth.

"Indeed!" exclaimed Mrs. Rawley, leaning forward to present the distinguished clergyman a view of her décolletage.

Mama sat quietly; only a small frown between her eyes and the O of her mouth, forming a silent "shhh," signaled agitation. Then in a near whisper she said, "I was raised Quaker myself, Sir, where women have spoken openly on their views these two hundred years."

The Englishman, however, ignored these interruptions and turned toward me, eyebrows drawn tight over cold gray eyes. "Beware, Young Lady. You are ignoring your Creator's plan." Then, his brow smoothed, and his mouth smiled: "I shall pray, Miss Evelyn, that you may be delivered from your sins."

Who asked him to intervene with God in my behalf? Not I! I took a deep breath. The room was intensely still.

Possibly a second or three had passed. I felt it as a great expanse of time. I did not recognize my voice, which sounded as cold as my insides felt hot. "Don't trouble yourself, Sir, or God, either. Your prayers would doubtless do more harm than good."

Papa's voice broke my concentration. "Sir, my apologies. Evelyn is perhaps too young to be included at table yet. Evelyn, you will beg pardon before you leave."

"I will not!" I whirled and pushed the tall carved back of my chair, expecting the satisfying *smack* of wood hitting floor. But Sapphire had moved behind me, and caught it.

"Child." Stone-faced, she signaled with those brilliant blue eyes, so striking, always, in her brown face.

"Child. Mind your manners."

I'd been inexcusably pert—in fact, rude.

I took a deep breath. "Mama, Papa, I apologize for upsetting your hospitality."

I marched from the room, back straight.

When I finished growing up, I'd prove that a woman could do all a man could do and still be a true woman!

Five

In Which I Fail
to Enlist Daisy,
but She Recruits Me

I JERKED my dress up with one loop of hoop and rushed up the staircase with petticoats exposed. Even so, my heel caught a ruffle and I clutched the banister in panic. *How will I ever get out of these contraptions?*

Daisy was waiting in my room. It was the first time she'd been there to help me undress. I'd made fun of Cousin Virginia for needing a "lady's maid," but now I was grateful.

"Daisy, what an awful evening! And then I ripped this."

"Mammy said you'd need me," she said, hiding a grin, "and you surely do, at that. Now simmer down, while I get these thingummies out of your hair. You'll feel better then."

She gingerly pulled each hairpin from the Edifice, which held together a spell, then cascaded onto my shoulders. Every strand was a misery as it reversed in its socket.

"Did I hurt?" she asked as I winced.

"You were gentler than Mama when she put it up. I reckon my hair has to get used to going backward."

"Lots to get used to, looks like," she said, tackling the hooks and eyes, then easing the dress over my head. A firm push in, and out again, released the crinoline, and—at last!—she jerked the corset laces, emptying alternate hooks.

I groaned with relief when she finished, and then pulled my nightgown over my head. "Oh, Daisy. What a day. I'm in trouble." I patted the bed, inviting her to sit. "Come listen."

"Can't, Miss Evelyn. Must put your things away proper-like." She spread the dress over the chair as Isabel had. "I'll ask Mammy about this. Never dealt with silk before." She folded the corset and camisole and fitted them in the top of my chest of drawers.

My heart sank. *Miss Evelyn.* Even worse from Daisy than from her mother. "Daisy, don't call me 'miss.' Please!"

She kept her back turned, pretending to sort the drawer. In a muffled voice she said, "Got no choice, Miss Evelyn."

She faced me with a serious expression. "Mammy says don't hunt up trouble; just do what we need to do."

"But—at least sometimes—what a person *needs* just naturally does court trouble. Don't you see that? Tonight, that man—that minister—he said women have no use except bearing babies. And then Papa said it was good that Mama was educated because that made her useful to him and the school. And learning was good for girls because it made us more worth marrying. As if women are only worthy if men get some good out of them."

I began to sob. "And then that miserable clergyman shook his finger at me and said I was sinful. And only Mama objected, not very loud, either. And then Papa ordered me to apologize! Men are terrible!"

The silence stretched out. I looked up. Daisy was still gazing at me, serious as before.

She sighed and ran a hand over her head. "Miss Evelyn,

Mammy and I would be glad to have my pappy and my brothers back, men or not. If we had that, would we worry about who was getting the good out of it?"

Though I'd known about Daisy's father being sold down river as long as I could remember, I'd never before discussed him with Daisy. Her face reflected a sorrow deeper and older than my indignation. I suddenly saw the transaction in a new light.

"That was awful of my great-aunt Jane, Daisy. Evil."

Daisy nodded, without comment.

As Papa had explained it to me and my sisters, Aunt Jane had reluctantly sold Julius in order to pay off her debts, so Uncle Carter would inherit the rest of her estate debt-free. I'd accepted the story uncritically, excusing the sale as a necessary act. Now it seemed repulsive.

"How could Papa let that happen?" I asked, as the reality of Sapphire and Daisy's loss sank into my mind and conscience.

"Marse Landon couldn't help it. My pappy, he belonged to Miss Jane and was supposed to go to Marse Carter when she died."

She shrugged, then faced me, determined. "And not just Pappy. We miss Dan and Eli, too."

Daisy's brothers, fifteen and seventeen, had run off months ago, and never a word since.

I stared at Daisy, and she at me. My stomach, despite its release, felt in danger of upheaval. "Daisy, I heard Liza's father tell Papa he could get the boys back with a reward."

Daisy's look made me wince. "We don't want them back in chains with whipmarks, Miss Evelyn. We're glad they've gone North. We miss them though." She pretended to straighten the drawer again. "I never met my pappy, but I miss him, too. Doesn't matter he's a man."

I slipped off the bed and padded barefoot to the bureau. Yesterday I would have hugged her without thinking, but now . . .

"Daisy?" I coaxed, touching her shoulder. She began to shake, and I put my arm around her waist and led her crying to the bedside. "I'm sorry. I'm sorry."

"Not your fault," she said, hugging back. "Like Mammy said, we do what we got to do." We sniffled together, on the bed. Suddenly, I sat up straight. "Daisy! Will Sapphire leave us—or you?"

Daisy shook her head. "Leastways . . . not soon. If Pappy gets free, this is where he knows to come." She rushed on: "Besides, Mammy wouldn't leave your mama. Mammy's for sure the best midwife in the county, and the best herb-woman, too."

A new fear rose within me—and yet, not so new. I'd begun to notice how drained Mama looked when she thought nobody was watching. I'd caught her smoothing a blush of rouge on her cheeks with a rabbit's foot, and she'd sworn me to secrecy. She didn't want even Papa to know she was a "painted woman."

"Mama shouldn't have more babies, should she?"

"She should not. Mammy told Miss Felicity even before Annalee, and after Beatrice she told your papa. Mammy says unborn babies just naturally take what they need; it's the mama who suffers. Your mama's been losing out, regular, these fifteen years. She needs to conserve herself."

Suddenly, Daisy looked alarmed. "You won't tell anybody I said this?"

"No, I won't. But why, Daisy, why? Papa loves Mama! He'd never harm her. So, why do they keep having babies? Especially if it hurts Mama? Why won't anyone tell me?"

Daisy looked away. "Best I can figure is, grown folks like making babies." She turned back resolutely and added, "But Mammy says there's another reason, too."

"What? What could be that important?"

"Old Marse Justin's Will. Strange things in that. But what keeps your mama having babies is, he left the plantation to your papa for life, and to his oldest son, if any. If there's no boy, then your cousin Dabney gets it when your papa dies."

Daisy stared at her lap. "Your mama and you girls wouldn't get much." She looked up. "I'll be in bad trouble, if you tell. You're not supposed to know all this."

"I can't believe Mama and Papa never told us." I stared at Daisy in true befuddlement. "They've told us other things about his Will, and Aunt Jane's Will, too. Why not this?"

Daisy twisted her apron between her hands. "I'm not real sure. Could be your mama and papa want you always to think well of Marse Justin and Miss Jane? Maybe don't want you worrying over things you can't cure? Or could be they're scared Nelly'd be tattling about losing everything if your papa died. Any husband of one of you might wind up supporting the whole batch."

"That'd drive off beaux, all right," I agreed.

My mind raced, skittering from the sale of Sapphire's husband Julius, to Grandpa Justin's Will, which sounded neither fair nor sacred. Even the image of bosomy Cleopatra in my grandfather's library windows rose to unsettle my former beliefs.

My whole view of Justin and Jane had shifted with a single day's twist, like the designs in a kaleidoscope turned. The colors as before—but the pattern utterly unlike.

———

THERE was no punishment when Mama came up to say good night to me and Daisy. She looked weary, but only said, "My dears, I wish I could give you a more just world." She smiled a pale ghost of her dimpled glory. "All I can do is see you both get book-learning and manners, so you can become a Light to the world wherever the Lord may see fit to call you."

"Mama!" I began.

She held up a hand for silence. "I don't hold with the Reverend's views, Dearest, you know that. But, they are not uncommon; many—even most—educated people believe as he does." She tried to smile. "You can't indulge in outbursts like that. Not if you wish to be accepted in society."

In her earnestness, she slipped into Quaker speech. "Darling, thee *must* learn to hold thy tongue. Thee was not only rude to a guest tonight, thee said things that, spread abroad, could harm thy family."

I wasn't sure how that could be; how could anything I said cause harm?

———————

LYING in bed that night, I pondered the evening's events. I was puzzled by my parents' passive acceptance of the Reverend's views on women and on slaves. After a bit, I set that inquiry aside as an oddity springing from adulthood—mysterious, but possibly, in time, understandable.

Daisy's information consumed more thought.

I'd always known Julius had been sold, but Daisy had somehow concealed the pain his loss had caused her family. And she'd never before wept over her missing brothers.

Her information about my mother's health had confirmed my own fears. But it had also increased my irritation at my father, who *knew perfectly well* that babies should stop coming.

Most puzzling was my parents' decision to keep their children ignorant of important terms of our grandfather's Will. I turned Daisy's suggestions over in my mind, but somehow they didn't seem sufficient.

Then, the truth burst upon me.

My parents wanted a boy. They needed a boy. They kept trying to have one, even at the risk of my mother's health. And they didn't want their girls to guess what a disappointment each one of us had been. So they kept silent. I knew they loved us, but, I now thought, as they might love a defective child. They must have looked in the cradle each time and thought, "This is ours, and we love her, but *she can never be what we'd hoped for.*"

My knees drew up of their own accord to ease the knot in my stomach, and I curled in a ball—too sad, too mad, too appalled, to cry. I could never admit to that discovery; it would only hurt my parents and sisters as much as it hurt me.

In Which I Absorb
New Views on Marriage
and Anticipate Goddesses

DAISY was Negro, which disqualified her for bosom friend. My official confidant was Liza Wright, younger sister of Win, the boy who'd caught me staring at Cleopatra.

Liza was six weeks younger than Daisy and I, but the most woman-like of the three of us. Her family's plantation adjoined our own, our friends over three generations.

Would I have been close to Liza if we hadn't been together from the cradle? I can't guess. But Liza was, in her own way, a wonder to me. And fun. There is nothing so reassuring as a friend who is an unrepentant sinner. One's own flaws seem less heinous.

It was Liza who'd once smuggled cigars, and later brandy, from her father's library for us to test under the magnolia. (Sapphire had quietly cured us on both occasions.) It was Liza, too, who had sneaked her mother's rouge pot, to practice painting our faces like actresses and huzzies.

The morning after my birthday, Liza rode over early with her brother, in order to chat before Mama's classes. We customarily started later than the boys did, as Mama first had to meet with her staff to plan the day's work for the Academy and plantation.

Ordinarily, Win parted company with his sister as they entered our property. Today, he rode up to the house and waved before trotting off. I waved back, pleased to be acknowledged by this Superior Being.

"Well, look at you!" Liza exclaimed. "Nelly told me the birthday plans, but I never expected this! My, my—your hair! And your waist! I do declare, Miss Chamberlyn, you are a sight for sore eyes!"

"I'm not best pleased," I said, glancing down at the cotton frock Pearl had altered to accommodate my new underpinnings. "The corset pinches, my hair hurts, and I only get to wear Greataunt Jane's locket on occasions anyway."

Liza swung from her sidesaddle and threw the reins to Josh. She tossed Toby a leather bag of mail. This often came to Wright's Rest to be relayed to us. "Here, Toby, mail for Marse Landon and Miss Felicity. Mind you take it right to them and then put the pouch back in my saddle."

She turned to me, with that sly sideways glance she used when teasing. "No wonder Win rode into the yard. He wanted another look at you, I reckon."

She watched me blush, and giggled. "Really, Evvy, you look ever so much more lovely, quite more than passable."

I was gratified to hear this, pale praise though it was.

"You've won an argument for me," she continued. "I told Mama about the silk dress and hoops in front of Papa, because Mama's been saying I must turn sixteen to come out. Which I could not have borne!

"However," she rattled on, "I knew Papa would come to my

rescue, and so he did. Mama and I are off to Richmond to out-fit me for my own appearance into society." She made me a stately curtsey, swishing an imaginary ballgown with one hand, extending the other for an imaginary kiss.

"So you'll have a corset and crinolines in six weeks?"

"Oh, before that!" She giggled again. "Now that Mama has shopping to do, she's eager to start. It will be fun above any-thing! Mama's already written your aunt Emma, asking if we might stay. Do beg to go, too."

"No."

She looked hurt; to soothe her, I added, "I can't buy as you do, Liza. I'd only get jealous, watching you become a fashion plate."

"Oh, poo," she answered. "You and your sisters—*and* your mama—are the envy of the county. She's got such a Frenchified touch with a pattern. Even my mama admits your mama has *style*, if a bit prim."

With a certain pride, Liza added, "Mama hasn't the least tal-ent as a dressmaker, let alone our Bessie." She gave me a sudden, delighted squeeze. "At last, I shall escape these homemade, schoolgirl clothes. I've cut seventeen pages out of *Godey's Ladies'* magazines to show to dressmakers."

"Liza," I said, "I like a pretty outfit, too, but these underpin-nings are painful. Females are kept in a terrible bind with these hampering clothes."

"Nonsense!" she said. "One has to suffer for beauty. Adjust your attitude or you'll never catch a husband." She slid me that teasing look again. "Win was quite taken with the new Evvy, I as-sure you."

She ran ahead and began to make herself giddy with

twirling, then bounced onto the horse-mounting block, and looked down. "I'll buy a new riding habit! I'm at my best on a horse, and I vow Dabney will notice me!"

I stared. Dabney? Mean old Dabney who teased his sisters and mine until they cried? Dabney, who might one day turn us out of house and home?

My horror showed. Liza leapt from the block and shook me by the shoulders. "Evvy, don't wear a sour face; I'm talking about flirting, not marrying." She cocked her head and grinned. "Dabney's not a bad sort. And he does like to ride as much as I do. If you'd endured a brother his age for years, as I have, you'd like your cousin better."

She put a finger in her cheek and pretended to consider. "Come to think, Dabney's well connected, but hardly rich enough. Mama says it's as easy to fall in love with a rich man as a poor one. Or even a medium-rich one, I'd guess.

"Cheer up, Evvy. You are so dull today!" She twirled again. "I'll tell your Richmond relatives that your trip to Philadelphia has ruined you, as they predicted."

I made a face. "Virginia and Georgia aren't inclined to think much of me in any event. Nor I of them."

Liza shrugged. "Georgie's a pest, but Virginia can be fun. Believe you me, if *I* had a cousin in Richmond, I'd cultivate her friendship." She narrowed her eyes—a look I knew meant business. "Now, you stay on her good side, Evvy. For my sake, if not your own."

She searched her pocket and extracted a page from *Godey's Ladies'* showing a bevy of Beauties in gowns. She tapped one. "See, this is labeled 'charming for the young debutante.' What do you think? Will it do for the Academy Christmas Ball?" She looked, suddenly, quite anxious. "Now that we're old enough to dance, I intend to be ravishing." We ascended the stairs to the Big House. "Virginia and I shall send poor Georgia quite wild with envy, I promise you!"

I believed her. Georgia would swoon over every frill and flower the older girls bought. Even I felt a twinge of envy. If I had to become a lady, I should rather be a Belle than a Wallflower.

We entered the morning room, where Mama assorted the usual papers and books on the table for the day's lessons.

There would be three daughters from Tall Oaks plantation, who came twice a week, and five girls from the nearby village who came four days a week. Ages ranged from seven to sixteen. Annalee, at four, might attend for an hour or two. Mama managed the flow. We all learned, despite the seeming chaos.

Today, she was reading a letter so intently that she didn't see us enter.

"Who's that from, Mama?" I asked, as Liza and I began grouping the dining chairs around the table.

She glanced up. "It's from your aunt Honor, with exciting news! She writes that Atha and Sophie want to visit for the next year and help teach the girls' school. Would you like that?"

"Oh, yes!" I breathed, hardly daring to believe such fortune. Atha and Sophie, Honor's daughters, seemed to me so beautiful and brilliant that my time in Philadelphia had been spent in dazed hero worship of them.

I turned to Liza, but she was already jumping with glee. "Lordy, lordy, I'll get to meet the Goddesses!"

It occurred to me that perhaps I'd bragged on my cousins over-much in the weeks after we'd gotten back.

"The Goddesses?" Mama asked, laughing.

"Well, that's how I think of them," Liza replied. "The way Evvy takes on, they're beyond mortal maidens in looks, brains, and accomplishments." She swooped her hem around her with one hand, while waving the other. *"And* mannerly, *and* wear their clothes with flair. And, of course, those names. . . ."

Mama and I exchanged a glance and giggled.

" 'Atha' does resemble 'Athena,' Greek goddess of wisdom," Mama admitted.

"And 'Sophia' means 'wisdom,' " I added.

Mama glanced at her letter again. "Honor and Paul believe Atha could profit from a change. She's been teaching in their school for five years and should see more of the world."

"And Sophie?" I asked. Sophie was only seventeen, even lovelier than her older sister. In fact, she was nearly a copy of my own mother, with the same beauty and natural gaiety. She had taught, but not officially—more in the way I taught Daisy, Josh, and Toby. Should she "see the world," too?

"She'll accompany Atha," Mama said, oddly abrupt. "Young ladies mustn't travel alone."

What else had Aunt Honor written?

Mama glanced back at the letter. "Honor adds that her girls should learn bookkeeping, and the business side of teaching." She paused, and explained as she read, "She wants Sophie to see what marriage and a young family demand of a woman. 'Let your nieces do nursery-work and household-running as well as school-marming.' "

I felt a surge of gratitude toward Aunt Honor. She'd seen Mama's frailty and thought of everything: help with teaching, with bookkeeping, with household chores, with child-raising. Like Mama, my Quaker cousins had grown up cooking! And sewing!

"How soon?" I asked.

"Probably in about six weeks. In mid-October."

I gave Mama a great squeeze, squashing the letter between us. "Papa will agree, surely?"

When she nodded, I grabbed Liza and she and I spun around the room, bumping chairs, causing the corset to dig into my ribs and the Edifice to topple askew. "The Goddesses are coming!" we chanted as we twirled. The misery of yesterday rolled off me.

The noise of the coach from Tall Oaks pulling up in front interrupted the celebration. Mama finished stacking the books on the table, as the first three students came chatting through the door.

As Mama greeted the newcomers, her dress brushed the letter unnoticed from the table, and the worser part of my nature sprang forth. I scooped it up and slid around the door frame into the pantry, while Mama explained about the new teachers.

An excited babble began, then my next three sisters joined the class. The news was repeated. I wasn't missed.

I scanned the letter, skipping to the meat of it.

They should be a real help, my Dear Sister, and it may save Sophie from a Disastrous Union. The young man is a Birthright Friend, so she would not be written out of Meeting as Thee was, but he is very Wild, and she is very Young. His parents are no help. They want the Match, and I can understand that. For my boys I'd want just such a Bride.

Aha! Theophilus. Theo. The young man whom Sophie had somehow met up with whenever she and I walked out alone, was a serious suitor. I'd obliged her by trailing behind as they whispered, and I'd promised not to report their meetings.

Sophie had admitted to me that her beau had fought a duel.

"Not a quarrel of his seeking, mind you. But he wouldn't back down." Now, that *was* somewhat scandalous, clearly un-Quakerly—but not excessively wild by Virginia standards.

The noise in the other room assured me my absence was unremarked. I turned the page.

I do think it is more than a Mother can Bear to see daughters Marry. We all have to stand it, but surely not my Sophie, so Young, and to someone so Unstable. There is Sacrifice in Marriage for women, or we should not feel so about it.

Did Mama, indeed, "feel so about it"?

The students from the village now arrived. I had a few seconds more. I skimmed the lines.

Though Thee and I have had Happy Unions, it is an awful Risk for a Girl. I should not wish my daughters not to marry, yet it will be a sad day for me when they do. At least, I should wish that Sophie, like Atha, would take her Time. Atha understands, Sister, and will be most responsible. Thee must . . .

I slipped through the pantry door, tucked the paper down a fold in my skirt, to slide silently onto the floor behind Mama's back. I headed for my own chair, my mind whirling.

Sacrifice in Marriage. An awful Risk for a Girl. Yet my mama and aunt seemed, indeed, to have happy unions. I'd never realized they saw, as I had begun to, the drawbacks to wedded bliss.

I opened a book and stared without seeing as I pondered more of the letter's surprises. *Mama had been written out of her Meeting for marrying Papa.* I'd never heard that. Why? This much I knew: Aunt Honor and Uncle Paul ran a school for boys and girls, where Mama had been a pupil. Papa taught there after he'd finished his degree at Harvard, to get experience for the Academy he had dreamed of starting.

That this had caused a commotion on the Virginia side, I knew from Sapphire. Old Justin had expected his son to come straight home. "He snorted around, stomping and swearing he'd never raised his son 'to waste himself teaching a pack of harum-scarum brats.' But Miss Jane hushed him up, and then he brought home your mama." Sapphire had chuckled at the memory. "Marse Justin took to her, so it didn't matter she had no dowry. He still thought he was rich, then."

No dowry. Why had I never wondered about that? I'd known Quakers admired a simple life, and I'd just assumed Friends' marriages didn't involve dowries. But I'd recently seen that my Philadelphia relatives all lived very comfortably indeed. I knew my mother's brothers had inherited substantial property after my grandfather's death, and Aunt Honor had mentioned that her home—a handsome house with a second building behind it for the school—had been her parents' wedding present.

If Mama were cast out of Meeting for marrying an Episcopalian, did that mean her papa had to disinherit her? Was that why Mama and I made the Philadelphia trip only after her father died?

My family on my mother's side had just slipped sideways in the kaleidoscope, too.

In Which We
Furnish Classrooms
and Face Danger

"MY DEAR," Mama announced to Papa at dinner, "we must provide a classroom and living quarters for Atha and Sophie."

"Why, they can use this room for lessons and the guest room for sleeping," Papa replied. "They're family, after all."

Mama raised her eyebrows in surprise. "Landon, we are getting their services free. Surely we owe them proper spaces to work and live."

She added, "The old kitchen building would work. Lessons on the first floor, living space above. Close to the house, but not underfoot." She smiled that special smile she used to persuade him. "And, Dearest, with a real classroom and teachers, we could admit more pupils and charge regular tuition fees."

"Well," Papa pondered, "it's possible. I checked the building only last month. It's sound, though rough."

Isabel piped up. She was perishing to meet the glamorous Goddesses. "Papa, our cousins mustn't live in a nursery. Why, Joycelyn and Annalee would drive them distracted, if they couldn't escape." She frowned. "We must make them comfortable."

Joycelyn began to retort, so I kicked her and shook my head. She jumped, then kicked Annalee, who swallowed her own protest. For once we were single of purpose. We all wanted our cousins to stay as long as we could keep them.

Mama signaled for quiet. "Even more important is a classroom." She looked around the morning room, and added, "How lovely it would be not to store books in the pantry, and not to remove schoolwork to serve meals."

Papa raised startled eyebrows. "I never thought, My Dear. Don't you prefer teaching in your own home?"

I rolled my eyes toward Sapphire, who ignored me.

"No, Landon, I can't say that I do." Mama rose, and moved to stroke his shoulder. "You know how well the old plantation office works when I take care of Academy business. I can keep the books open, the files in view, and work in peace away from the children."

She smiled at us. "Not that I don't enjoy my home and my girls! But order and quiet let me finish quickly and return to them." She turned the dimples on Papa again. "The old kitchen would work equally well for a school. We'd have growing room, quiet hours in this house, and," she added, squeezing his shoulder lightly, "privacy for us as well as Atha and Sophie."

Papa was convinced. In the end he recruited ten workmen, led by Horace and Dr. Williams's Jethro, a fine cabinetmaker. The Negro crew labored through September. They covered the dirt floor with pine planks, while Jethro constructed two-person desks complete with benches.

Bookcases and cabinets rose against the walls. Mr. Wright donated a modern stove that sat in the middle of the room and was vented with black piping up the huge old open chimney.

The ladderlike steps to the upper floor became a staircase; wood was sanded, old walls were replastered. Horace supervised the division of the upper floor into a sitting area and two bedrooms, and Mama and Isabel and I furnished them from our attic storerooms.

The Williams girls' doctor-father contributed a set of leatherbound volumes of philosophers, and Susan Stewart's lawyer-father donated a fat dictionary with its own ornate oak stand.

A great slab of slate took the combined strength of the men to attach to one wall, while a large, new map of the world decorated another.

We girls went several times a day to check on progress. Of all of us, I was the most thrilled, for I was the one who knew our cousins. I suspected that Sophie, pretty, sweet natured, and so like Mama, would be the general favorite, but it was Atha I anticipated most.

Atha: the only female I knew who rarely dwelt on household matters—men, babies, clothes, recipes, and such. Even the drabbest household duties became easy with her around. Once, for instance, we were darning her brothers' socks. All one can say in favor of darning is, it saves knitting a whole new sock. And Atha had four brothers. We faced a long afternoon.

A spool rolled off a table, which reminded her of Newton's apple. Then she remembered an article about gravity, where objects of differing weights had been dropped from the Leaning Tower of Pisa. That lead to discussion of Italian architecture. By the time we finished, we were discussing the Pantheon. (One can see the stars at midday through the hole in the dome!) I was actually sorry to fish the last sock from the sewing basket.

I could hardly wait to have her as a *real teacher*. With the extra advantage of daily cousinly chats.

Excitement reached a fever pitch as October, and our cousins' arrival, approached. One morning, Papa announced a dedication ceremony for the new school. Mama was surprised, but pleased.

Quite a crowd gathered before the building at noon: our servants, the men who'd worked on the job, all the girl students, Mr. Wright, Dr. and Mrs. Williams and their coachman, and Mama, of course. Papa stood on the stoop, started with prayer, then praised the workmen and Mama, who, he said, was now headmistress of a real school. He then nodded to Horace and Jethro, who came forward with a wooden plank, turned to its blank side.

"It has come to my attention," Papa announced, "that our young ladies have high expectations of their new teachers."

He paused for effect. "In fact, I understand they are termed 'The Goddesses.'" He grinned. "Therefore, as a real school must have a name, Horace and Jethro have created a final touch to improve the premises." Here he gestured toward the two men, who grinned back.

They flipped the board, which was beautifully carved and painted with the words

MOUNT OLYMPUS CLASSES FOR YOUNG LADIES.

There was a gasp, a giggle, an outbreak of applause from the crowd, and a whisper running through the servants after Daisy explained the sign. I could see that Mama was a bit embarrassed, but that Mr. Wright and the doctor were laughing with Papa. *That's all right,* I thought, *we'll show them. We'll be a credit to the name.*

As the crowd broke up, I grabbed Daisy, and we ran to catch Horace and Jethro. "Please, before you leave, could you do one more thing? I'd like the smaller black slate and the old map put up in the back cabin."

"Sure enough. Be glad to, Miss Evelyn," said Horace. "Even that littler slate is downright heavy."

"Where-at do you want them?" Jethro added, as I led them to the side of Olympus, where the old slate leaned against the wall.

I peered around the corner. Dr. and Mrs. Williams and their girls were still chatting with my parents. "Don't go this way," I cautioned. "Best circle around and go in the cabin from the back, so the Williamses won't see us."

Daisy said, "You go say good-bye; I'll show them." The men hefted the slate; I handed Daisy the rolled map, and they quietly rounded the rear of the row of slave cabins.

Though Papa had razed several of these cabins for their bricks, most of the two facing rows of quarters stood as originally built. Sapphire and Ruby occupied three cabins each; Horace had added porches to connect bedrooms and parlors. Only Pearl had elected to stay in the Big House, in a room off the kitchen. The remaining six cabins were boarded up. Or appeared to be.

The one closest to the woods was my schoolroom, where I taught Daisy daily, and often her cousins as well. The shutters opened easily, and inside were a sturdy table and chairs, books, and several small slates.

My parents pretended not to know. The law forbade teaching Negroes to read and write, but Mama had first taught Sapphire's sons, and then Daisy and me. Then the Wrights begged her to take on Liza; soon other families asked, too. So Daisy got learning secondhand, from me. For six years or so, there'd been no problem.

I trotted back to wave farewell to our guests. The village carriage had already left, and the Tall Oaks coach waited for the dust to settle before following. Liza, splendid in her new riding outfit, mounted to go home.

Nelly spoke up. "Liza, if you go that way round, you might catch Cousin Dabney. He was asking for you. He and his friend rode that way." She pointed toward the row of cabins.

"Dabney? What's he doing here?" I asked.

Papa spoke up. "Carter wrote me that the Spottswood boy'd offered Dabney a ride from Richmond, to get a bit of hunting. We had a vacant bed in the dormitory, so of course I said yes."

Papa kept hoping his nephew would attend his Academy, but Aunt Emma wished to keep him home as long as she could. A fine plan, to my mind.

My parents gave a final wave as the last vehicle lurched down the lane, then they walked toward the house.

"Why would Dabney ride that way?" Liza wondered.

"Well," said Nelly, with that air of importance I loathe, "I told him you were at the old kitchen, but if he didn't see you there, he could try Evvy's school."

"What!" I exploded.

"You always yell at me!" Nelly crossed her arms and pouted. "I only told him I saw you and Daisy heading toward your school, where you teach her and Josh and Toby. He and his friend said thanks, and rode that way. I thought Liza would be with you."

I turned and ran toward the cabins, panting against the corset. As I went, I heard Liza's mount behind me. "Stop!" Liza yelled.

"Can't," I gasped.

"Silly, I know about the cabin! Stop a minute!"

I slowed and looked up at her.

"You can't take on Dabney alone. Especially with that

Spottswood boy. Win says he's a bounder of the worst sort." Her face was as flushed as when we smoked cigars. "I've known about your school forever, Evvy. Who gives a hoot, so long as you keep it quiet?" She smiled. "Dabney may need to be reminded that no *gentleman* would tattle on his own kin."

She made sense. Dabney wouldn't care about me, but, since Liza's shopping trip to Richmond, she'd giggled about attention he'd paid to her. She'd seemed quite cured of him, however, now that she considered him a conquest.

I trotted beside her, easing the corset a bit, until we spotted two horses tied to a tree. She dismounted, handed me her crop, then tied her horse and took a similar whip from one of the other saddles. She brought it down hard against the tree trunk. Her eyes sparkled. "Just in case," she said.

I nodded, and we moved toward the cabin. What would Dabney do? Complain to my father? Threaten the law unless we stopped? Have his father intervene? Liza and I sidled up to the window and pulled the blind out a little.

What we heard, I could not believe.

It was Daisy's voice, begging, pleading. "No, no, Marse Dabney! No! Don't! Please! I'm gonna scream! I'll tell!"

"Go ahead, Nigger. Scream. Nobody's around to hear," said a voice I didn't know, one thick with excitement.

"Spotts, maybe we shouldn't," said Dabney's voice. "Her mammy's not any old Nigger; my aunt and uncle listen to her."

"They won't dare do nothing," the other voice replied. "Look at this. They've been letting Niggers learn to read on their land. They go after us, we go after them. My pappy'd jerk me out of this Academy if he knew 'bout this."

"You think so?"

"I know so. Other parents would, too." The boy laughed, a

low, ugly sound. "We could empty the school *and* sic the law on them. They won't tell."

There was a tearing sound, and a scream from Daisy.

I jerked away from the window, Liza behind me, and headed for the door. I swung it wide, and it whopped back against the outside wall, letting the sunshine in.

Daisy stood full in the light, holding her torn bodice against her chest; the boy I didn't know suddenly dropped her arm. Dabney whirled, put his hand in front of his face, and tried to dash though the doorway.

Liza stuck out her foot and tripped him. He sprawled, then rose to his knees. "You miserable worm," she said.

"Daisy, are you all right?" I asked.

She didn't answer, only clutched her clothing and took a sobbing breath.

I advanced on the other boy, who seemed frozen in place.

"What do you think you're doing?" I was amazed at my own calm. "Answer me!" I brought the riding crop across his waist, sharply, and he jumped away, making an astonished *yip*.

"This has nothing to do with you," he said. He turned to the doorway. "My God, is that you, Miss Wright?" He pulled a kerchief from his pocket and began to mop his face.

He walked toward the door, his brow now wrinkled in concern. "Miss Wright, I'm appalled you should have been exposed to this. Pray, let me escort you home."

Liza drew back. "I should not have been exposed had you not behaved badly."

"Believe me, neither Dabney nor I would ever have led you into such a situation." He leaned to help Dabney up, and eyed his dusty trousers. "Better brush yourself off, Old Man," he said. "You need a bit of fixing."

A whimper escaped Daisy, then she, too, ran for the door. Liza and the boys drew back, and I saw her uncle Horace catch her in his arms. Her gasping little sobs wrenched at my innards. I moved to the table and sat down hard.

We could hear Horace: "Ran for help, fast as I could, when I saw them, Honey. Couldn't hit those rascals myself. Worth a Black man's freedom to do that." His voice and her sobs faded as they headed down the row to Sapphire's cabins.

"So he came for me," a different male voice boomed.

The handsome Mr. Rawley, Master of Latin and History, once the amateur boxing champion of the College of William and Mary, loomed in the square of sunlight. The shadow he cast on the cabin's dirt floor was long and menacing.

Eight

In Which I Begin
Collecting Secrets
of My Own

"I AM appalled. I am ashamed to call you my scholar, Spottswood." Then Mr. Rawley turned to Dabney. "What would your father and uncle think?"

"But, Sir . . . ," Dabney began.

"We were just checking out this Nigger school," the other boy said. "Surely you didn't know this was here? You wouldn't support going against the law, I know."

"This I do know," Mr. Rawley said. "You were harming another man's property, and your behavior has injured two delicately reared young ladies. You should be ashamed." He paused. "You cannot escape demerits, Spottswood. I'll consider your punishment. As for you, Chamberlyn, you'll leave for home tomorrow. I'll not broadcast your disgrace, so long as neither of you speak of these events to anyone. Anyone! Do you understand me?"

"Yes, Sir!" both boys chorused.

"Get out," Mr. Rawley ordered, and they dashed for their horses. He watched them leave, then turned and noticed me. "Miss Evvy, are you all right?"

"No." The dagnab corset, designed for sedate ladies, now took its revenge. I gasped to force air down to my lungs, but the pinch in the middle left no room. As the air went down, breakfast came up. I began to retch. Liza scooped up the waste bucket and held it thoughtfully beneath my chin, only barely in time. Suddenly, her own face went white, she thrust the bucket into my hands, and—not at all gracefully—she fainted. Another victim of corsetry.

Though Mr. Rawley had seemed powerful before, he was ill suited to handle vomiting and fainting young ladies.

He stared at Liza, who was flopped on the dirt floor, ran a hand through his hair, looked at me, looked back at her; sighed. He muttered something—maybe *Oh,myGodwhatnow?*

I knelt beside Liza, and shook one shoulder. "Liza! You all right? Answer me!"

She groaned; "Evvy?"

"You hurt?" I asked, beginning to pull her up.

Mr. Rawley cleared his throat, and Liza started. She'd forgotten he was there, and now began to readjust her skirt.

"I can keep those ruffians quiet," he volunteered, "but you two must decide *now* whether anyone else can know of this."

"Shouldn't we tell Papa?" I asked.

"No!" said Liza and Mr. Rawley at the same time.

"No!" said yet another voice. I turned to see Sapphire in the doorway. "Pardon, Marse Rawley, but may I speak on this? Daisy's my own child."

Mr. Rawley bowed slightly in Sapphire's direction. "Of course. I'm glad we agree."

She paused. "That Spottswood boy, he's pretty near to being White trash. Bet his pappy has him here to be a gentleman. If

Marse Landon throws him out, he'll tell who-knows-what story to the world. But, if he stays, he keeps quiet."

"Just what I think myself, Sapphire!" exclaimed Mr. Rawley. "In fact, when Spottswood Senior left his son here, he hinted that he hoped his boy would become friendly with Win Wright. So he could then court Win's sister."

"Ugh. No," said Liza.

I nodded. "Spottswood was mighty concerned over Liza. 'Let me escort you home, Miss Wright,' and such stuff." I saw Liza shudder. "Never you mind, Liza. He may guess you despise him, but he won't want his father to find he's ruined his chances."

"Exactly!" exclaimed Mr. Rawley. "Also, if he or Dabney still have hopes in that direction, they won't want your reputation sullied, my dear Miss Wright. Or yours, of course," he added, as an afterthought, nodding to me.

"That's all right," I said. "I know she's an heiress and I'm not. But . . ."—I giggled as I considered—"that probably means I need to be *unsullied* even more than Liza, to get married."

A raw noise cut through my merriment. Sapphire was crying.

"Sapphire!" I ran over and hugged her.

"Let go, let go. I've got to go to my baby. My poor baby." She pulled herself from my arms. "You—laughing about *sullied* and *unsullied,* what do you know? Nobody touched you."

"Sapphire, oh, please, I'm sorry. Please."

Sapphire returned the hug. "Forgive me, Honey. I'm glad you helped her." She turned to Liza. "Owe you thanks, too, Miss Wright." She nodded to Mr. Rawley, her usual dignity restored. "And you. Owe you thanks, too." Then she slipped through the doorway and was gone.

Liza frowned as she watched Sapphire leave. "Dabney we could have handled, I reckon, but that Spottswood boy is another matter." She gave her sunniest smile, and curtsied toward Rawley. "Thank you, Kind Sir."

He did not respond, but looked grim. "He's a danger. As Sapphire said, he is *not* a gentleman. I can control him, but only as long as he fears his father."

"What about Dabney?" I asked.

"When all's said, your cousin *is* a gentleman. He knows the rules, and he has his family's reputation to protect. And, speaking of reputations," Mr. Rawley continued, "I must advise you to keep this a secret." Seeing my face, he added, "Miss Evelyn, I'm not protecting these young men, but you and Miss Wright and your father's school."

"He's right, Evvy." Liza had finished pulling her clothing into order. She now removed her strangely tilted hat, brushed it vigorously, and resettled it at the correct angle. "We'd best get in shape. My parents will be looking for me."

She marched to her horse, mounted, and turned to me. "Do you have my crop?" she inquired.

I scooped it from the ground and handed it over.

She leaned to take it, winked, and said, "My, my, Miss Chamberlyn! And I used to think 'twas I who lured you into wicked ways!"

With a gay little wave of her still-kid-gloved hand, she was off across the fields.

Nine

In Which the Goddesses
Settle In
and Unsettle Me

OUR teachers arrived in mid-October, shortly before the presidential election of November 1860. Horace met them at the depot with the carriage, and he drew up with a flourish before Mount Olympus. Atha and Sophie hardly waited for him to lower the steps before tumbling from the coach to hug Mama and exclaim over the rest of us.

My sisters and I flocked around our cousins, toting small things, stampeding up the steps onto the old kitchen's front porch.

"Oh, my," said Atha, admiring the sign that read MOUNT OLYMPUS. "How shall we ever merit such an exalted address?"

"That's because you're the Goddesses!" cried Annalee.

At this, my cousins dissolved in laughter. Sophie's nose wrinkled when she laughed, and it wrinkled now. "When I name children, I'll be kind. No goddesses."

Atha moved to the doorway, laughing. "Shall we go in? I've always wondered what the abode of the Olympian gods would be like."

"Me first! Let me!" shouted Nelly, shoving aside Annalee and the toddling Beatrice. The baby, two weeks into walking and now in short skirts, plopped onto her plump bottom and started to howl.

Sophie scooped her up and bounced her. " 'Tis only thy pride is hurt, Babykins. Come, Sweeties. We'll all go in together."

We helped to settle them in. Isabel and Nelly exclaimed over their modish but quiet-colored clothing, while I shelved their books and gloated over as-yet-unread treasure.

An atlas, histories of England and France, three identical volumes of *Caesar's Gallic Wars* in the Latin, and a tome containing etchings of Greek ruins were among the display. It was the entire shelf of novels, however, that promised hours of excitement: works by the Brontë sisters and Jane Austen, *Ivanhoe, The Last of the Mohicans,* and suchlike titles. Papa's library did not run to fiction, but the occasional treat I'd borrowed from Liza's mother had whetted my appetite for more.

——◆——

IN no time at all, our world changed. Girls my mother had not had room for now enrolled. The school turned profitable. Mama was thrilled that her prediction that the school would make money if properly set up had come true. Every so often she would remind Papa of this over dinner. To his credit, he simply twinkled back. "With three genuine goddesses in command, how could Olympus fail to succeed?" he'd reply.

Atha had a gentle but firm way of exacting compliance. The students now came daily. On time. "Teaching and learning require consistency," said Atha.

Sophie began a nursery group, with Annalee and Beatrice and the five-year-old sister of Susan Stewart. Mama was freed from baby care for the first time in years. "Women need time to themselves," said Atha.

Daisy helped with the infants, then slipped into the rear of the room during Atha's classes. She appeared to be there to run errands, if needed, but even without pencil and paper she absorbed more of Atha's lessons than most girls. At night, she taught Josh and Toby.

My cousins were sympathetic when I told them of my school, closed for fear of discovery. "Thee can tutor for me, Evvy," Atha said, and assigned me the girls who had problems in group learning, regardless of age. The slower ones I helped to catch up; the advanced ones I kept from boredom and mischief. This way, I was kept from boredom and mischief myself.

An unexpected hubbub arose when two foundlings were abandoned on the porch of Olympus in as many nights.

One midnight, Sophie heard what she thought was a cat in distress, but found a baby in a basket. She and Atha brought the infant to Pearl's room off the kitchen and insisted she rouse my parents immediately. We all got up and rushed around finding Bea's outgrown baby clothes, while Ruby made a teat for the child to suck, of butter and sugar wrapped in a clean rag.

The next evening my cousins found a second child, this one a toddler, tied by a leash to the doorknob of Olympus when they went back after dinner at the Big House.

"Oh, please, let us keep them!" Sophie begged. But Papa arranged to deliver the children to the county poorhouse.

"The matron there is kindly," Papa said, "and the children are well fed and clean. When they're ready to be put into service, I'll see them well placed. I can't do more."

That seemed harsh, yet I understood. My younger sisters had taught me how much work every new baby makes. My conscience, however, told me that as a *woman* I should not let such practicalities influence me. I should be upset over the babies as Mama and Sophie were, rather than agreeing with Papa's male view of the matter.

I spent several evenings before the children's departure at Olympus. Sophie's distress was easier to endure than my parents' parlor, where the atmosphere was decidedly tense. I also felt better about my own lack of female virtue as I watched Atha cope with the dilemma.

The final evening, Atha insisted on carrying the babies to Sapphire, and then tucked Sophie in bed early. The two of us sat in the schoolroom talking as Sophie sobbed herself to sleep upstairs.

"Atha, what do you think?" I asked.

"Your papa's right," Atha said with a sigh. "We cannot run a proper school if we become an orphanage."

I pondered this. "Atha," I asked, "do you love children?"

"Well, I love some, as I love some adults. And I hope I feel Christian charity for all. But I'm not constituted to adore every child, as Sophie and Aunt Felicity do," she replied. "In fact, that is one of several reasons I don't expect to marry. How awful it would be to spend years raising a child one disliked!" She chuckled, and added, "After all, there is no telling—one's child might take after its Black Sheep uncle instead of its sainted grandmama."

"Then, how do you manage to teach the girls you don't happen to like?"

Atha gave me the smile of a co-conspirator. "Evvy, thee should understand if anyone does. Thee's no more inclined than I am to love the world, but thee does love learning. And teaching, too, if I'm not mistaken."

I gulped, and my face burned. I felt exposed. It was true.

I was fondest of Josh and Toby when teaching them, yet I loved Daisy all the time. I cringed to be so uncharitable.

Atha saw my discomfort and gave my shoulders a light hug. "We get our natures from God, Evvy, and should not apologize for His work. Consider," she continued, "though people expect all women, especially teachers, to adore children, this is unreasonable. Nobody expects it of men."

She frowned slightly. "In a boys' school, irritation and dislike toward students is considered normal; even beatings are not rare. Women, teachers or not, are people. We have as much right to evaluate students—even to dislike obnoxious ones—as male professors have."

I nodded, but my uncertainty must have showed. Surely good women loved everybody?

"I, for instance, should go mad without teaching," Atha said. "And I don't much care to whom. I'd teach crones mathematics, urchins embroidery, and monkeys to fly, if nothing more sensible offered itself."

We giggled together, and I did feel better. Atha's view of life suited me far better than the clergyman-lecturer's did.

I entered the Big House hallway in good spirits, only to hear Mama's voice rise in anger. My parents were still arguing about the foundlings. "Landon, it is hardly the poor babies' fault that they are the result of adultery."

"You're right that they're probably by-blows," Papa said, "or they'd not be cast aside like this. But, Felicity, this is *not* punishment for their parents' sins; it's a purely practical decision. If we keep these, more will turn up. I cannot finance an orphanage." Papa's voice rose, and the parlor door banged shut, a sign my parents were engaging in a rare quarrel.

By-blows. My mind mulled over this word. It meant nothing to me. But *adultery* did sound familiar. Why, of course, this was one of the Thou Shalt Nots given to Moses on the Tablets of Stone. I had heard sermons on the Ten Commandments, but nothing explaining "adultery."

As soon as I reached my room I consulted my Bible.

The Commandments about killing, stealing, lying, and honoring parents were understandable. Adultery remained an enigma.

Though it was late, I slipped down the back stairs and tiptoed into Mount Olympus. The dictionary stand had two candleholders, and even stubby candles, which I lit from the taper I carried. I flipped to locate the word.

> **adultery,** *n.* violation of the marriage bed; a crime,
> or a civil injury, which may introduce into a family a
> spurious offspring. Sexual intercourse of any man with
> a married woman; but of a married man and an
> unmarried woman is fornication in both, and adultery
> in the man.

How anyone could violate a bed, criminally or civilly, was unclear to me. *Sex,* as in *women are the fair sex,* I knew. But *sexual,* obviously an adjective or adverb, was a mystery. *Intercourse* I had heard, but the idea of social visits between neighbors and friends did not fit here.

I flipped to the Fs.

> **fornication,** *n.* the incontinence or lewdness of
> unmarried persons, male or female; also, the criminal
> conversation of a married man with an unmarried
> woman. ADULTERY. IDOLATRY.

The best I could make of it was that some kinds of conversation between persons of the opposite sex could be criminal, as some attacks upon beds might be. *Adultery* was no help as a definition, and *Idolatry* confused me completely. I thought it meant bowing down to false gods, an entirely different Thou Shalt Not of the Ten Commandments.

My whole inquiry seemed hopeless.

Suddenly, Atha's voice broke the silence. "Evvy, what is thee doing?"

My heart jumped to my mouth. "N-nothing," I fibbed.

"Of course thee's doing something," said Atha, descending the stairs. "Nobody scans the dictionary at this hour for nothing."

"I . . . um . . . was just reading the Bible, and . . . um, well . . ." The more I explained, the more embarrassed I got; by the time I choked out "intercourse," I faltered to a halt.

Suddenly, Atha began to laugh, bringing Sophie to the top of the stairs. Even from there she sensed my embarrassment. "Stop, Atha. Thee's upsetting her."

"She . . . she's wondering about *intercourse*," Atha gasped. "Remember when thee did that, too?" She hugged me, and stifled the merriment. "Never mind, Dear. We all wonder."

Sophie gave her a severe look. "And Atha's going to tell thee about it, right now. Just as she told me. Is thee not, Atha dearest?" she added in a sweetly mocking tone, as she beckoned us up the steps.

Sophie and I settled on their divan, where she tucked an afghan around us for warmth. Atha donned her dressing gown, lit an oil lamp, and pulled a book from hiding in her trunk.

"Here," Atha said. "My father bought medical texts from a doctor's widow for his library. Mama wouldn't discuss these matters, but felt we should not abide in ignorance, so she gave us this book."

Sophie flushed slightly. "We have helped raise brothers. What's in this book may be even more surprising to thee than to us."

The next half hour was one of the most informative of my life. The book seemed hardly believable, but the engravings were graphic, and my cousins would not lie. Dazed, I said, "You mean my parents have done this . . . thing . . . *six times?*"

Atha began to giggle again.

Sophie frowned. "Stop poking fun, Atha." She turned to me. "People enjoy it. If they love each other," she added hastily.

"They do?" I asked.

Both cousins nodded.

"That's supposedly so, in a proper marriage," Atha said, but her lips were tight. I didn't feel she believed it.

"What if someone doesn't like it?" I asked.

"Well, if thee is married thee is obliged," said Atha. "The Bible says 'be fruitful and multiply,' so it is God's will that babies be born. But people who aren't married mustn't do it."

"But the dictionary said . . ." I halted.

"Exactly which words did thee examine?" asked Atha.

"Adultery, first." I blushed. "Then something that began with F."

Atha took a deep breath, turned pink, and plunged ahead. "Adultery is when a married person does this with a nonspouse. The other word must be *fornication*. That's when neither person is married at all."

They watched as I thought. "So the Bible forbids adultery, but not fornication?"

Atha looked at Sophie in a silent plea for help. This subject was, I gathered, an exception to her claim she'd teach anybody anything.

"Well," Sophie offered, "adultery is always a breaking of a vow. Fornication isn't so bad. It might actually amount to a pledge. At times. I think."

Atha shook her head firmly. "Don't mislead her, Sophie. God and Society condemn both. Children born out of wedlock are called bastards."

"Love child is a nicer term, though," Sophie muttered.

Suddenly, the scene with Daisy holding her torn dress against her chest rose to my mind. "What . . . what happens if a not-married person forces another not-married person to do it when she's saying 'no'? Suppose there's a baby? Is it a bastard?"

Atha's brows drew together. "The Bible says the sins of the fathers are visited upon the children. That seems harsh, but it is, I fear, true. Such children are not socially recognized, and even our laws disinherit them."

"It is most unfair!" Sophie broke in violently. "Innocent children should not suffer because their parents sinned!" Her eyes brimmed with tears. "A woman forced is innocent, too, surely."

Though I'd sworn not to tell anyone, I found myself spilling the story of the attack on Daisy to my cousins.

Atha was stunned that we'd kept the incident secret. "We must go to thy parents tomorrow, and thy papa must expel this evil from his school and turn thy cousin from sin."

Sophie objected. "Atha, thy meddling may lead to harm. This Mr. Rawley had sound reasons to advise secrecy."

Atha stood, and handed me my candle. "It's time we all go to bed. We must pray about this tonight."

Well! You can imagine how much I slept! The physical act sounded amazingly uncomfortable, and I no longer wondered at

Atha's decision not to marry. The result of this strange act was, apparently, babies. Sinful or not.

I would have to warn Liza and Isabel and Daisy—oh, oh my! My head whirled, and in the few dreams that came, I rode the nightmare.

I woke in the morning knowing I must get Atha to listen to Mr. Rawley, embarrassing though that might be.

Ten

In Which I Begin
to Accommodate
to Ladyhood

IN MID-NOVEMBER we held a tea party to introduce Atha and Sophie to the neighborhood and Papa's faculty, even including the Academy housekeepers.

Mama announced this last decision while Mr. Wright was visiting, and Papa demurred. "The Jenkinses will feel out of place, and our neighbors might object."

Mama smiled at Mr. Wright, and replied, "Our friends have tolerated my eccentricities for years. If they can accept a married schoolmarm, they can surely sip tea with plain women who earn their bread honestly." She put a hand on Mr. Wright's sleeve. "I'm counting on you and Patsy, Winston. Where you go, the rest will follow."

"I warrant you'll have a full house, Landon," Mr. Wright predicted, slapping Papa on the back. "Not a soul in the county that hasn't heard of your Goddesses. My Patsy is perishing of curiosity, and she ain't the only one. Felicity could invite ten farm women to tea without losing a guest."

He grinned at Mama. "Now, serve that special pound cake, you hear? I plan to come watch the fun, though I've had the honor of meeting the young ladies several times."

In fact, most of the male members of my parents' circle of friends had managed to ride by to discuss something with Papa and thus satisfy their curiosity, while their ladies were condemned to stay home until invited.

Liza told me it was thought a great shame that my cousins were Quaker, and thus held a quiet Meeting of their own instead of attending Church where they could be examined. And, of course, nobody could invite them to visit before they were properly introduced.

"However," Liza rejoiced, "that's to my advantage; I'm the center of attention since I know most about them—other than family, of course, and you can't be quizzed."

———

ONCE Mama had sent invitations, she, with Sapphire, Ruby, and Pearl, cleaned corners, waxed furniture, and shined silver. When Atha and Sophie insisted on joining the orgy of housecleaning, Mama loaned them two of her voluminous aprons to protect their clothing.

"What a wonderful invention," Atha said, as I did up the ties marching from neck to waist.

"It's Mama's design," I said. "She's worn it to teach in, too, when . . . you know . . . she's 'increasing.' " I blushed a little, even knowing Atha would not get flustered. "Chasing after babies is easier without stays, too," I added. "Mama sometimes leaves them off underneath."

"I believe I'd put a full closure in the back," said Atha, turning before the mirror to get a rear view. "Then one wouldn't need a dress beneath." Atha shook her head. "Poor Sophie! She deals with sticky fingers and grimy feet all day!"

Atha examined herself again, and smiled. "It's not scandalous, like Mrs. Bloomer's creation with the Turkish pants. It's as modest as a gown. I'll write Mama to send us dark calico from Philadelphia. That'll hide dirt and wash easily."

As Mr. Wright had predicted, guests were plentiful and prompt. By late afternoon the event had reached its height. Every carriage came crammed with guests, from the Stewart girls' aged grandmama to the newborn from Tall Oaks.

My sisters slipped through the crowd with other young children, filching cookies and punch. For a time, I felt obliged to watch them; but, as Isabel took over, I slipped off to test the pleasures of my first adult party.

It was exhilarating to join the clusters of gossiping ladies who had formerly shooed me away or reminded each other that "little pitchers have big ears." The silk dress and the formerly despised corset magically transformed me into a member of the female adult circle.

I hovered briefly outside the library, but of course I couldn't invade the gentlemen's lair. Though this event was officially a "tea," Papa, with Horace to help, was dispensing bourbon punch to his friends.

Everyone seemed in the mood for a party. This tea was a fine diversion for the usual lull in social life between the summer barbeques and the festivities of the Christmas season. Liza had vowed to flirt outrageously, and I meant to watch her. I crossed the yard, expecting to find her in Olympus, where my cousins were playing hostess.

Ancient Mrs. Stewart, supported by her granddaughter Susan, shuffled through the school on her cane, marveling at the warmth from the stove. "In my day, we learnt our ABCs and samplers by firelight at home," she said. "This is very fine."

Her sparrow-bright eyes peered greedily at the shelf of

novels. "I can't see close-to, but our Susan's been reading your *Jane Eyre* to us of an evening. We're all atwitter with wondering what will be next!"

"Susan's welcome to borrow more," Atha said, turning to me. "Don't let me forget, Evelyn, to lend Susan another."

"Have you finished the first volume of *The History of the Decline and Fall of the Roman Empire*?" a male voice asked, and I realized Mr. Rawley had joined our group.

"Oh, Mr. Rawley, I cannot thank thee enough!" Atha turned quite pink with pleasure. "If the other volumes are as informative, I shall be set with reading matter for the entire winter. I've wanted to read Mr. Gibbon's work for years."

Old Mrs. Stewart patted my arm, and prepared to shuffle back to the refreshments. "Send me that next book, now, Evvy. Come, Susan, keep moving. I need to set meself awhile."

Mr. Rawley gave a parting bow to the Stewarts, then turned back to Atha. "It's my pleasure to share with a kindred mind," he said. "Would you be interested in discussing Gibbon's ideas? A good book is improved by discussion, I believe."

"Oh, I agree!" said Atha. "Perhaps we could form a literary group to meet occasionally." She looked as if to include me.

But, before I could speak up, Mr. Rawley added, "That might take a while—finding people with both desire and time to read so long a work. May I trade you a new volume in a few days? We could explore the earlier period while it's fresh in your mind."

Atha hesitated, but said, "I would like that."

She looked down and flushed slightly. In a low voice she added, "My thanks again for your aid to my cousin"—she nodded toward me—"and to her friend and Daisy. Your counsel was immensely helpful, and I know the subject was as difficult for you as for me."

"Oh, *there* you are, *Caro Mio*," Mrs. Rawley called from the doorway, where the magnificent sweep of her hoop, some ten feet in circumference, quite filled the frame. She pressed the sides of her costume together, and oozed through the opening, progressing majestically toward our little group. She let her paisley shawl slip back to her elbows, to reveal a neckline lower than usual for afternoon.

"Must you schoolmarms and masters bore the rest of us with business?" She pouted prettily in the direction of her husband, then slipped her arm through mine. "We shall just have to punish them, shan't we, Miss Evelyn?"

She turned to Atha, adding, "I vow, you must let your little students have this afternoon to play, Miss Atha. All work and no play makes Jack a dull boy, you know. Come, Dearest, we don't want you turning into a dull Jack, now do we?" We watched them as Mrs. Rawley steered her husband back to the Big House.

Atha remarked, "They seem ill matched, but I understand that Southern men regard Bluestockings such as I am as unfeminine."

"Oh, no, Atha. Nobody could find you unfeminine. Or Mama, or Sophie, either."

I threw my arms around her in an enthusiastic hug. "All the gentlemen are enchanted by you. Mr. Rawley, especially."

Atha laughed a little. "Thee thinks so?"

"I know so." I hugged her again. "Why wouldn't he be? You're the smartest woman here, and nearly the prettiest! I want to be just like you!"

I tried to find an excuse for Mr. Rawley's poor taste in a wife. "Mrs. Wright says it's as easy to fall in love with a rich person as a poor one. Perhaps Mr. Rawley's mama told him that, too."

Atha smiled at the flattery, but she said only, "I would hate to think Mr. Rawley was mercenary."

I thought of the dinner party. "I think . . . I believe he's bored with her."

"I hope not. They are married." Atha turned to greet another eager pupil touring Olympus with her parents.

I decided to see how the other half of the party was progressing, and, to be truthful, to show off the "new" Evelyn.

Several ladies had exclaimed over how grown up I'd become. Two had actually complimented my tiny waistline. And the locket had been the subject of *Oo*s and *Ahh*s. I'd never been so much the center of attention.

In the front hall, Liza was practicing flirting with—of all people—the oldest Jenkins, while her brother stood by. Win rolled his eyes at me, as I entered, and, breaking away from his sister, slid his hand under my elbow, steering me toward the dining room.

"I cannot abide my sister in this mood," he muttered.

With exaggerated politeness, he added, "Miss Chamberlyn, you've not had your share of the delicacies. Let me bring you some."

He winked. "Lately, I've begun to admire women of substance." However, I noticed he was staring at my locket, which was, of course, substantially upheld by underpinnings—so, I supposed *substance* might not refer only to my intelligence.

I dipped my chin and looked up at him through my lashes, and—I vow it was as easy as anything—I was flirting! Soon I was even giggling. I sat in a corner, with my toes together and a napkin spread, and found myself conversing with a *boy*.

How we moved from the giggles to politics, I can't say. Win had visited the library and my father's bourbon punch. He was slightly tipsy, I believe, and bursting with opinions. Today,

I gathered, the senior Winston had brought news to share: The South Carolina legislature was expected to vote secession from the Union. In December! Only weeks away! Win sounded up-wrought over this, as men tended to get.

I cast about for response, and parroted my father.

"Well, but Virginia only needs to wait till the cooler heads prevail, as they must. South Carolina has threatened secession these forty years—but she's still in the Union."

Win paced back and forth, and would have trompled my hem had I not tweaked it back. "Just because we joined the Union doesn't mean we can't leave it. We do the work down here, and they skim the money off us up there."

Win slapped a fist into his other palm—one of his own fa-ther's fiercer gestures. "I tell you what, Evvy, those Northerners treat their workers like dirt. Fire them when they're old or sick. They don't give a hoot about Negroes. Slavery's just an excuse to boss the South."

I had run out of material on this subject, so I turned to one closer to my heart. "Do you class my cousins with the rest of those bossy Northerners?" I asked, practicing my eyelash flut-tering.

"By no means!" Win's gallantry was as recently acquired as my own coyness. We spent an amazingly agreeable half hour in teasing that would have sickened me six months before.

All too soon, the afternoon became evening. The party had been a success; the Quaker cousins had been pronounced to be, as advertised, goddesses among women.

Mama glowed with the righteous pride of a hostess who has triumphed over all rival events of the recent past. "Though Sap-phire is the heroine here," she declared. She and Sapphire hugged in mutual congratulation.

Atha and Ruby scouted for dirty dishes, while I dumped liquids down the drain and stacked the dirties near the wash basin; Pearl scraped plates into the pig slop as Sophie handed them to her.

Toby came to the back doorway, and fidgeted. I decided to make him useful. "Hi-ho, Toby. Go find more glasses and teacups. Get to work."

When he danced back through the door, muttering about looking for Mammy, I decided to corral him. I whipped off the towel I'd tied around my waist, dropped it on the table, and followed him down the back stoop into the dark.

I stumbled over something—no, some*one*—where ground should have been. "Oh!" My hoop billowed up in back, and my hands scraped the flagstones set into the ground around the stoop. My chief concern, on the instant, was my dress, silk being not washable.

I looked up, into a dark face. My eyes adjusted; more people, crouching silently, became visible. Strangers, all.

Toby's voice, whining out of the blackness, was the only sound. "But, Mammy, I did my best! I kept them in the bushes till the White folks left, and brought them out soon's I could."

"Hush your mouth, boy. You've got no more sense than a jackrabbit." The tone was harsher than I'd ever heard Ruby use. Not a single noise rose from the shapes near me.

Sapphire's hand went over my mouth, and her whisper filled my ear. "Come with me." She helped pull me up. "Come."

In another whisper, she said, "Ruby, you hide them. Next-to-last cabin. I'll be there soon."

She pulled me through the door of her parlor-cabin and pushed me into a fireside chair. "We've got to talk," she said.

Eleven

In Which I Am
Cured of Blindness
and Brave the Cold and Dark

I HAD been, to be blunt, blind. For years, the boarded-up slave cabins had been hiding places for runaway slaves. I'd never focused on the odd telltale thing I'd seen. Never wondered why Mama didn't advertise her dislike of slavery. Never thought why Papa pretended ignorance of my secret school.

Mr. Wright had warned my father of danger, but even he had no idea that my parents were assisting escapees—a far more dangerous activity than failing to advertise for fugitive slaves.

"After Miss Jane sold my Julius, I changed," Sapphire began. "Before that, I had no notion of joining the Railroad. After . . ." —she shrugged—"seemed it was the only thing helped my miseries." She shook her head as I tried to interrupt. "Now, Honey, you just listen; we don't have time to discuss.

"She was sneaky, was Miss Jane. Bedridden as she was, she bided her time. She knew your parents would kick up a fuss over selling Julius, so she waited till they left for a wedding. She sent for the slavers, handed Julius over. They paid a heap of money and took him right off. When your folks came back, Julius was three days gone, and the cash handed to the lawyer to clear her debts."

"Oh, Sapphire, how did you stand it?" I asked. I shook her wrist. "What excuse could she give for such a terrible thing?"

"I wouldn't say she excused. I remember exactly what she said to Marse Landon: 'That man was my property, and valuable. I had every right to sell him, and I did it in a way that kept my disabilities of age and sex from handicapping me. Rant as you will, 'tis done and over.' "

"Couldn't Papa have bought him back?" I asked.

Sapphire gave a deep sigh. "Miss Jane said no. She claimed not to know where the slavers went. She kept saying, 'I'm a dying old woman. And I've done right as I see it.' "

"Right! How could it be right to sell someone away from his family? And Daisy not even born!"

"Well, she didn't *like* doing it. But, she did feel she *had* to do it." Sapphire shook her head and sighed.

I stared at my hands, speechless for once. Then I asked, "Didn't you hate her?"

"For a time. But, Miss Felicity and me began helping folks go North to freedom. Seems like that eased the pain, and the hate, too."

Remarkably, she smiled; the firelight only partly created the glow of her face. "And one day my Julius will come through on the Railroad. I'll be here then."

She turned to face me directly. "Something I learned from this, girl. Anger has its uses, but hate's an evil thing. It eats the hater right up, and mostly doesn't hurt the hated."

I looked at her in wonder. Could I have loved her and her family if I'd been treated as she had? I doubted it. My stomach felt leaden with something. Guilt? But what did I have to do with these old, past injuries?

"Papa knows about the folks coming through?" I half stated and half questioned.

"Honey, I reckon most everybody on this place knows. My boys, Dan and Eli, took the Railroad to Philadelphia, to your aunt Honor. Miss Felicity visited them there. Didn't take you. Daisy knows, and even Ruby's boys. But children are risky. Josh is too young. He got fuddled tonight; we were lucky only you found out." She gave me a stern glance. "Don't tell your sisters."

"I won't," I vowed, and crossed my heart. "But Sapphire, I heard Mr. Wright tell Papa he'd inquired of the stationmaster, and the boys hadn't escaped on the railroad."

"Honey, you never heard of the Underground Railroad?" Sapphire shook her head. "Guess not. How would you, unless I told you, which I couldn't. What it is, is a whole bunch of different kinds of people who help slaves escape."

She stopped short. "I've got no more time for talk." We stood, and she patted my shoulder. "Don't worry, Honey, we've been at this awhile. We'll manage."

Josh appeared in her doorway. "Auntie," he panted, breathless with running and fear. "My pappy ain't here. He left with Doc Williams to help Jethro with a job."

His eyes were big. "Pappy was in the library with the menfolk all afternoon. He never heard about these passengers. Mama says what about Daisy?"

Suddenly I realized Daisy was missing. What with flirting and all, I'd not noticed.

Sapphire swayed, then grabbed a chair back for support. "Lord help me," she said. "What's next?"

"I can help," I said, "if you need me."

The look she gave me was appraising. Then she shooed Josh out. "Tell your mammy to keep folks calm. I'll be there soon.

"Come," she said, and I followed her to Dan and Eli's old bedroom. There, she rooted in a chest, saying, "I've been saving Eli's outgrowns for Josh. Should fit you."

She began to undo my gown and hair. "Put these boy clothes on. You'll be going through some rough stuff."

As I dressed, she spoke rapidly. "Daisy's built brush piles, but she won't fire them till she hears, in case something went wrong. Horace was busy today, so Daisy had to get the signal ready."

She shook her head. "Can't send Josh and Toby, they're afraid of ghosts. Nor your cousins, they don't know the way. Never send your mama or papa. I've got to calm that cabin full of folks and tell them what next. You're the best I've got, just now." She looked at my feet. "Can't wear those flimsy slippers, nor Eli's boots. Here." She kicked off her shoes.

She took a lantern from a cabinet and lit it; it was the kind that could be shuttered. "Keep it dark till you get to the woods. You'll need light then. You know the boys' swimming hole?"

At my nod, she continued. "Go along the path by Fat Creek, down to the huge flat rock. Call out 'Olympus' when you get near. That's tonight's password. Daisy will tell you the rest."

"Mama?"

"I'll let her know."

With no more exchange, I was away. The moon was half full, enough to see by in the park. In the woods, though, moonlight barely filtered through. I opened the shutter.

The path was narrow, with roots to trip my feet and branches to swipe my head. The lantern cast shadows that hid bumps and holes. At each stumble, I feared to drop the thing, burn myself, or face the dark alone.

Daisy and I had come here in summer, Joycelyn tagging behind. We'd even swung on the rope over the swimming hole, wishing we could go naked and plunge in as the boys did.

Then, we'd giggled with the pretended fear of discovery, and the path had been sun spotted under protective trees. Now I felt terror, cold and real.

The swimming hole was black and could have been any size; its far bank was invisible. Fat Creek was rightly named. It was wide, almost a shallow river. The path narrowed as it ran along the creek. I threaded my way toward the flat rock, ducking branches and pulling Eli's heavy trousers from brambles.

Finally—there the rock was. Its huge surface loomed as an opening in the woods. Moonlight glinted over it; the front end tipped down from the bank into the creek, reflecting like a frozen waterfall.

"Olympus!" I called.

Nothing.

"Olympus! Daisy! Olympus!" My voice cracked. I simply couldn't face going back alone.

Out of the dark came Daisy's voice: "Evvy? How come you're here? Where's Uncle Horace?"

Relief melted my knees and made the lantern wobble.

"Hey! Cover that light."

I shuttered the lantern and moved onto the rock, stumbling over its rough surface. "Where are you, Daisy?"

From a deep fold in the rock, a head popped into view. "Evvy. Be careful."

I came to the side of her hiding place, set the lantern down, then perched on the crevasse edge, my legs—in Eli's pants—dangling into the hole.

"You look funny," said Daisy. "How come you're here?"

"Horace left the party with Dr. Williams, and there wasn't anybody else. Your mammy sent me. All she said was to get here; you'd know what to do."

"Thank the Lord Jesus. I've been cold and scared." She pulled out of the hole and sat on the edge beside me. "First, we light the fire. Wait for an answer. Signal back. Then leave."

She walked with the lantern to the far edge of the rock. Dimly, I discerned a mound. Flame flickered; soon the brush pile blazed on the safe, flat stone. Minutes passed.

The blackness of the creek showed a bright reflection on a ripple or two; then, somewhere high, beyond the far bank, a lantern was unshuttered and reclosed four times in rapid succession. *Blink. Blink. Blink. Blink.*

Daisy returned the signal. She paused for perhaps half a minute, then began to blink in such rapid succession that I lost track. The other lantern signaled again. She scrambled over the rock to me. "Let's go," she said.

We slipped down the slope of the rock, and I followed her to the swimming hole and through the woods, until she doused the light at the edge of the moonlit park.

"What did all that mean?" I whispered.

"From the rock, the fire shows over the creek, through a break in the trees, to a house on a hill, where the next conductor lives." Daisy paused. "Somebody sits near the window from dark to midnight, peeking out. When the brush burns, they signal back, four blinks. Six blinks means it's not safe; keep the passengers another night.

"If they don't answer, we light the second fire for another

chance. After they signal, we blink as many times as the number of people railroading. Tonight's a big group."

I could see furrows of worry on her forehead. "I hope there's enough boats. It's cold, now, for wading through. I'm glad Dan and Eli left in warm weather. The journey isn't easy, even then. I'm glad I won't be going this way."

I hugged her. "I'm glad you won't be going, too," I said.

She leaned her forehead to touch my hair. "Not what I meant," she said. "I am going—someday—but not like this. Not running and hiding in the dark. Dan and Eli are coming back for me."

"When will they come?"

"Mammy says when they have the money and strength. When the Good Lord permits. Whenever." She shivered violently; her hand felt ice-cold through my sleeve.

"I'd hate for you to leave," I said, as I grabbed her hand and rubbed it for warmth. "You're frozen," I said. "Take Eli's coat."

"Nope." She shrugged off the suggestion. "We're near done. Let's get home fast." Holding hands, we scuttled across the park to safety and comfort.

Atha huddled near Sapphire's fire. She leapt up and said, "Go to Sophie in Olympus. She has your clothes, Evvy, and a warm tub waiting for the two of you. I'll tell Sapphire."

———

A HALF hour later I entered the Big House in full party dress. My parents sat in the parlor. Papa closed his eyes in visible relief when I entered.

"Did thee have a nice evening?" Mama inquired. "Chatting over a party is half the fun, I've always said. Thy sisters wished to join thee, but Papa ordered them to bed, giving thee privileges of the eldest."

"Thank you, Papa." I went forward to kiss them. "This has been an interesting day," I said.

Papa put an arm around each of us and kissed Mama, then me, on the forehead. "You're as tall as your mama, now," he said. "Almost a woman." He tightened his hug. "These are complicated times. I want to keep all my girls safe and happy. Pray God I may, with honor, do that."

Mama gave him her special smile. "Dearest, women must heed their Inner Light as men do. This is hard on papas, but Evelyn will choose her own path, as I did when I married you."

The mischief twinkled in her a moment, and she added, "Patriarch you may be, but you are so outnumbered that you'll have to accept petticoat rule sooner or later. Best adjust now. By the time Beatrice is my height, you will be an old hand at setting daughters loose."

Twelve

In Which I Discover My Quaker Roots and Mrs. Stowe

CHRISTMAS approached. The main event was the Ball, to be held in Chamberlyn Hall the evening before the boarding students left for family celebrations. Aside from hiring musicians and sending invitations, not much could be done until the day before the festivity.

In the meantime, we amused ourselves with secret present-making.

Nelly was in a fever of excitement, embroidering "Christmasgift" on needlecases and bookmarks. We all knew exactly what we'd be getting from her, but we tried to keep our own secrets. She was notorious for nosing out every hiding-place and spoiling every surprise before December twenty-fifth.

Isabel was doing something with flowers she had pressed flat in her Bible during the summer, provident as she was. She turned pink with indignation each time Nelly poked and pried.

Joycelyn required Horace's help, and spent time in the quarters, coming home smelling of fresh pine and whistling like a boy. Nelly and Isabel banded together temporarily in disapproval.

I went to Wright's Rest, where Liza and I cut up old issues of *Godey's Ladies'* to create pictures for my sisters, and for Liza's mother and aunts. We tinted the gowns with watercolor, glued the designs to thin wood backing, and bound the edges with braid from old gowns.

For Papa, I planned a fair copy of the beginning of the Declaration of Independence, decorated with hand-drawn eagles, which I also glued and bound. For this job, I spent several evenings with my cousins, perfecting my handwriting at the round table in their parlor.

While I wrote, and rewrote, my cousins told me more about the Underground Railroad and Mrs. Harriet Beecher Stowe. Which was the more astonishing I can't say.

First, Atha explained the Railroad. "It has nothing to do with rails or boxcars or regular depot stations. It's the business of hiding escaped slaves: midnight journeys, back stairs, priest holes, and songs with double meanings are the usual equipment."

"What goes underground?" I asked.

Sophie laughed. "Not much," she said. "An occasional tunnel's been built from a cellar to a safe place, and I hear that caves are sometimes hideaways. Mostly it just means *secret*. One man even got mailed in a box from Richmond to Philadelphia; he was on the Underground Railroad and the real railroad at the same time."

"He was upside down half the trip," Atha said, "but he made it through in health. The White man who took the box to the train was fined and imprisoned, when his part was revealed." Her lips narrowed. "There are scoundrels called bounty hunters who track slaves and return them for rewards, dead or alive, as if they were animals."

I knew, of course, that aid to escaping slaves could end in prison for a White person, in whipping and branding for the slave. "Why do people, White or Black, take that risk?"

"Thee did, thyself," Atha pointed out.

"I never thought about it, though. Not like nailing a man into a box and posting it. I mean . . . it's just not worth jail."

Atha went to her trunk again, this time producing *Uncle Tom's Cabin*. I'd never heard of it. As I wrote, my cousins read chapters aloud.

I argued at first that the book was ludicrous. Nobody I knew would treat his or her people so badly.

My cousins reminded me of the sale of Julius and the attack on Daisy. "Thy own family has done such things," said Atha. "Think what other people, with less conscience, may do."

"Everyone in the North has read this book," Sophie added. "I admit, I myself hardly considered slavery until I did, though our Quaker Meeting has been a Station on the Railroad for years."

"Well, our Meeting has a long history. Circumstances change, and different people need help." Atha put down the book and asked, "Do you know about Indian Annie or Mam'zelle?"

"No. Were they slaves, too?"

Atha shook her head. "No. But they needed help." Her face lit with that "teacher look" I loved. "Thee should learn about our side of thy family. Quakers call themselves Friends, you know. For good reason.

"When our mama was about ten, she was walking one evening to Meeting, when men raced by, carrying torches and yelling about the 'Indian witch.' She ran to Meeting with the news, and when the Quaker adults arrived at Annie's hut, the mob was about to set fire to her straw roof."

Atha's eyes widened. "The Meeting surrounded the ruffians, chanting psalms, and Grandma moved to the front of the group, holding your infant mama, followed by the other ladies and girls."

"Why?" I asked. "Wouldn't men do that?"

"Well, no." Sophie broke in. "Quakers avoid violence. The babies unnerved the rabble. They broke ranks and slunk home." Her nose wrinkled with amusement.

"What happened to Annie?"

"She became quite a favorite of the Meeting. She was a wonder at concocting cures. Mama adored her, and Annie taught her about herbs. Mama wrote the formulas down—which was a hard job. Annie had no more idea of names or measurements than Sapphire has about her concoctions."

Atha pulled a home-sewn booklet from the trunk, titled *Herbal Healing, or Indian Annie's Receipts*, in Aunt Honor's handwriting. "We'll copy this for thy mother."

"Did she know Annie, too?"

"Yes. But Mam'zelle was Aunt Felicity's special friend. Your mother was also about ten when she found Mam'zelle collapsed in an alley and brought her home. She'd escaped the guillotine and numerous uprisings in France, only to become a refugee in America.

"So," Atha continued, "since Grandpapa believed everyone needs work, he paid the woman to teach your mama French. Which is why your mama is so fluent."

Sophie giggled. "He didn't know Mam'zelle was raised in a convent school famous for needlework. She also taught Aunt Felicity to fit muslin patterns to a model, free of charge."

She leaned toward me confidentially. "Mam'zelle used to say, *'Zee good Jesus, He would never demand of ladies zee poor fit.'* And, after Mam'zelle took our family in charge, the females developed an un-Quakerly fashion sense. Grandpapa held her responsible for what he called 'Felicity's lightmindness.'" She sighed, "Mine, too, I suspect. Aunt and I are much alike."

With a guilty grin, she whispered, "Mam'zelle even taught me dancing!"

"What happened to her?" I asked.

"She became a well-known dressmaker."

"Well," I said. "How romantic. Imagine saving a witch, or rescuing a victim of the French Revolution!"

"Thy own adventure with Daisy was quite dangerous enough," replied Atha. "One's Inner Light can detect God's will in any time and place, and there's always new work to be done."

I looked at Atha, almost in despair. Her approval was so important, and yet I had to be honest, at least with my cousins.

"I really don't worry much about slavery," I admitted. "I'm glad to have helped when our own people needed me. But . . . but, this Inner Light you and Mama talk about—it just doesn't seem to shine in me. I've not worried much about those Railroaders. I'd never turn anyone in, but I surely don't feel as Daisy does."

A moment of silence followed this confession. Both my cousins rushed to talk, then stopped, waiting for the other.

Atha started. "Thee must follow thy own Light, dear Evvy. 'Tis not sinful to ignore another's Call, however just that Call may be. Myself, I feel a thirst, both to learn and to teach, that I dare not deny. The certainty of the Call makes me trust it is my Inner Light moving me. It is the certainty that convinces."

Sophie blushed, then made her own confession. "I feel called only to marry and raise a family," she said. "I would help an escaping slave if our paths crossed. But I cannot"—she looked at Atha—"I *cannot* dedicate my life to scholarship, or emancipation of slaves—or indeed, any other Cause—and be true to myself."

She blinked, looked down at her lap, and added, "I miss Theophilus so much."

A sound escaped Atha, something between a "no" and a "shh."

Sophie's chin went up. "Well, I do. I promised to take this year to think, and not to contact him, but I never vowed to forget him."

We were all quiet for a time. I had never realized that sunny-natured Sophie was hiding such a lonely heart. I would have liked to be sympathetic, but didn't want to upset Atha, as she clearly disliked the topic.

As I hesitated, Atha broke the silence. "Sometimes I think, what can I do? Or you, Sophie? Or you, Evelyn? What can any woman accomplish in this world?" She sat, suddenly, very straight. "And then I reflect: Mrs. Harriet Beecher Stowe, *one woman*, wrote a book and, if the Union does break apart, *one woman* will have done much to create that break."

"For good, or for bad," Sophie said, softly, "one woman has made a difference." She spoke, more softly yet: "No one could write so eloquently without guidance from her Inner Light. That book must, in the end, be for good."

On that note, we ended the evening. I gathered my completed gift and bid a "good night," but did not forget the discussion.

From that night I gave serious thought to secession. Would our country indeed fall apart? And would one woman's words have caused the break?

It was no longer a man's issue I could parrot occasionally to impress a beau.

In Which We Discover
Helen of Troy

WE NOW looked forward to a seasonal event. Cousin Virginia and Uncle Carter were due to arrive from Richmond. This was an annual Christmas visit, but—most importantly—this year my cousin and I could take part in the Academy Ball, along with Liza and the other girls of the neighborhood who had put up their hair but were not yet married.

Usually the entire Richmond branch of the family came, with servants, for several weeks. My mother and sisters bemoaned the fact that this year only two of the Richmond family would be coming, but I knew their regret, though genuine, would be short-lived. Each year we were gladder to see them go than come.

Aunt Emma was at least twice as languid and four times as inclined to gossip as Mrs. Wright, without her sweetness of disposition. Virginia and Georgia's airs of superiority over their country cousins thinned their welcome after a few days. Usually Georgia's entertainment was left to my younger sisters, but as Virginia and I were almost the same age, her amusement fell to my lot. I was fortunate to have Liza living nearby, happy to join us. Cousin Dabney was less trouble: He ignored us girls when possible and escaped to ride at Wright's Rest with Win.

Uncle Carter was different, however. We all looked forward to his visits, Papa particularly. They were true friends and missed each other, though they argued vigorously.

So I told myself that we'd all enjoy my uncle, and that I could at least flaunt my locket before Virginia at the Ball. This is not the kind of pleasure one would prefer to get from one's cousin, but under such circumstances, one does the best one can.

The change in the usual plan was due to a silly childhood disease. Dabney and Georgia were stricken with mumps. Aunt Emma could not leave them, but Virginia refused to miss her promised treat, so she and her father would visit for the Ball, at least.

"If they can't all come, why do I have to endure Virginia?" I fumed at Liza, as we stared through the parlor windows to glimpse Uncle's coach. I knew better than to say such things where Mama or Papa could hear.

Liza had never felt as I did about my cousin, but now she surprised me. Her eyes narrowed, and she balled her hands into fists and stuck them on her hips.

"Now, you listen to me, Evvy Chamberlyn. Don't you go riling up Virginia. Your uncle made it *plain as day* that my chance of staying with them in Richmond for a Season depends on Mama bringing us *both*."

It was true that Uncle Carter, like Papa, wished all of us cousins to be devoted and thought long visits would help. And true, too, that Mama would never linger in Richmond, while Liza's mother would adore spending several months chaperoning parties where marriageable young people could meet. And Aunt Emma, left to her own desires, would never agree to launch me into society with Virginia—partly from rivalry, partly from indolence, but mostly because she disliked me.

However, if her dear friend Patsy Wright were willing to bear the difficulties of escorting young ladies to various functions . . . ah, that would be different. She'd enjoy the company of a compatible guest and could also leave any inconvenient tasks to Mrs. Wright. I could understand Uncle Carter's plan.

I was not intrigued. "If coming out in Richmond society means tolerating Virginia for months, why would I do that?"

"Ninny! Of course you'll do it. We'll meet exciting new people—not just local boys, but men!—and go to parties—and have a new wardrobe."

I admit, the idea of a glamorous round of festivities was tempting. "But, I'd have to endure Aunt Emma and my cousins."

"You be nice to Virginia." Liza pointed a finger at me. "If you ruin my chances of going to Richmond, you're no friend of mine anymore!"

She flounced toward the door, but quickly returned. "I dasn't leave you alone. You'll mess things up for sure."

I shook my head again. "I'll behave. After all, this visit's only for a few days. I can manage."

I knew I should mend my ways.

Besides, I'd miss Liza dreadfully if she made good on such a threat. It was not a chance I'd willingly risk.

"Promise? Cross your heart?"

"Cross my heart and hope to die," I said, gesturing. "I'll treat her like a princess."

UNCLE Carter drove up in style, and Virginia waved with a glee matched by Liza. "High time," called Liza. "What kept you? We've been waiting these two hours!"

"Oh, you have no idea how tiresome mumps can be," said Virginia. She hugged Liza. "We took forever to get off. Dabney's truly sick, but Georgia kept whining to come. She feels fine; she only swelled up on half her face. Mama was changing my wardrobe to the last minute, until I thought I'd scream."

She turned to me. "Am I in the Blue Room again?" At my nod, she called, "Rebecca, take my luggage to the Blue Room. Unpack quickly; I'll want the yellow sprigged for dinner tonight."

"Yes, Miss Virginia." The voice was soft and ladylike, and I turned to see who spoke.

I was used to admiring beautiful women in the blonde mode, and mildly regretted my own coloring. So the young person who emerged from the coach amazed me. Her hair and lashes were nearly black, her eyes a startling gray, and her pale complexion glowed with a golden undertone that made me think of Spanish princesses or Scheherazade, the Sultan's bride from *The Arabian Nights*. She was the most beautiful female I had ever seen.

"*Who* is that?" I asked.

"Rebecca? She's my new maid," Virginia answered. "Papa traded Sally for her recently. Pretty, ain't she? *Very* good with hair, and trims a bonnet to perfection. Papa's friend got the worse of the deal."

Why would anyone trade this girl for Sally, who was homely, kind, and somewhat simple?

I looked at Liza. She raised her eyebrows and shrugged. The mystery here eluded us at present.

In Which the Mystery
Increases and
I Make a Rash Promise

LIZA and I went to visit with Virginia while she settled in. I sat quietly on the bed in the Blue Room, leaving the settee to Liza and Virginia. They chatted, as Rebecca unpacked and put clothing away. She was uncommonly graceful, as well as beautiful. It was hard not to stare.

After a while, Liza said, "Virginia, I saw every last item you bought in September, and I heard your mama declare you'd not get a *single new thing* till spring." She laughed. "Here, we're only at Christmas, and you've got stunning outfits I never laid eyes on. Tell your secret; I'd like to work your wheedle on my own mama."

Rebecca suddenly stood statue still, her face turned from our view, but she was clearly listening.

"Oh, these new outfits came with Rebecca, believe it or not," said my cousin. "Her first mistress spoiled her, you know. She was old, and doubtless dotty, for she'd laid away a trunkful of dresses labeled for Rebecca, which the girl claims she never knew. Mr. Montcure, Papa's friend who traded her to us, found it in the old lady's storage room when she died."

"How strange." Liza's eyes were round with amazement, and I'm sure my own were startled, too.

Virginia prattled on. "Rebecca's second mistress, Mr. Montcure's wife, naturally couldn't allow the girl to use them. She said even the clothes Rebecca'd worn in the old lady's house were quite unsuitable, and she donated them to foreign missions."

Virginia snickered. "She'd bought two servant's outfits to make Rebecca look respectable, and, when we traded, she insisted Mama reimburse her for them. Mama was furious!"

Liza nodded with fascination, murmured, "Oh, my," in an encouraging voice, and added, "the Montcures let Rebecca keep the trunk?"

Virginia nodded. "Well, anyway they passed it along with her. I suppose Mrs. Montcure had no use for the clothes, as they're not her style and her children are boys. Anyway," she continued, waving her hands in excitement, "when Mama took over the trunk, she saw the clothes were brand-new, modish, suitable for a young girl, and had never even been finally fitted."

"My, my," said Liza.

My cousin's voice rose with enthusiasm. "She just called her dressmaker right in and had them fitted to me. Which doubled my wardrobe."

She giggled. "As Mama said, 'those maid's outfits were a bargain after all.'"

I groaned inside to think I had relatives who were not only that base, but were stupid enough to brag on the "bargain" out loud. I blushed to have to face even Liza after this.

I looked for Rebecca, but she'd vanished.

I glanced toward Liza, and she toward me. What could she possibly reply?

She shrugged, and her eyebrows rose in the way that means, "There's nothing to be done about it." She turned back to Virginia and paused to think. "Well," she said slowly, "the poor girl could never wear clothes like *these* in her station in life. It would be a pity to waste such pretty things."

I jumped from the bed and said, "I know Mama must need help with the baby while she's organizing dinner."

Both the others looked relieved. Virginia probably wanted a heart-to-heart chat, and Liza needed time to digest this story and put the best face on it, before we talked.

By the window at the end of the hall, Rebecca stood. In the instant of hearing the door open, she slid behind a heavy drapery. I hesitated, then ran to the window, and whispered to the material. "Rebecca, Rebecca, please . . ."

The drapery stirred, but she remained hidden.

"I am *ashamed* to call that person cousin. I apologize for her, and I'd return your belongings if I could." I felt sweat on my brow from humiliation.

A few slender fingers curved around the edge of the material. I still couldn't see her face. "Miss Evelyn, please go. If she sees us here, things are worse for me. I know you mean good, but there's nothing you can do." Her voice constricted, with the effort of holding off tears. "Nothing anybody can do."

My old dislike of Virginia blossomed into rage. A fantasy of jerking my cousin around by her hair played behind my eyelids. I'd done that when we were five, and I'd never regretted it despite the punishment afterward.

I turned to leave, then turned back. Through narrowed lips I hissed a whisper: "I'll do something. I promise. I will." I had not the least plan in mind to back such a promise, but it had been made.

———

AFTER dinner that evening I tested my newfound ability to blend unnoticed into the adult world. Isabel and Nelly eagerly accepted Virginia's invitation to see her new wardrobe, and our cousin was happy to accept my excuse that I'd seen her clothes already. Soon Mama left to tuck the younger children in, by which time I had settled in with a book at the far end of the parlor and become invisible. Papa and his brother smoked cigars, sipped brandy, and in time told me all I wanted to know.

Uncle Carter was bursting with news and had brought the *Richmond Enquirer* with all the telegraphed details: South Carolina had left the Union yesterday, December 20. He predicted a landslide of other states would follow.

Papa read the news for himself. "I agree with the Mr. Pettigrew quoted here," Papa said. "He says, *South Carolina is too small for a country and too large for an insane asylum.*"

Uncle laughed, but replied seriously. "When all the lower South joins South Carolina, the confederation will be much bigger than any madhouse."

I took a quick glance, before looking down at my book. Papa had always been positive the Union would endure. But Uncle Carter's face was grim.

"Now, Landon, I agree secession's foolish, but I suspect it's inevitable." My uncle paused to draw on his cigar. "The real reason I brought Virginia wasn't because she teased me so about missing the Ball. I wouldn't have left Emma to cope with sick children alone, only for that. I need to talk plainly to you before you dig yourself a hole. A grave."

A grave?

"Most Virginians feel as we do, Carter." Papa leaned forward and flipped the ash from his cigar into the fire. "Or, at least I hope you're still of my opinion that the moderates can find common ground. That the Union will survive."

From the corner of my eye I saw my uncle nod. "I'm still far from joining the Fire-Eaters of South Carolina, Brother. I personally think they're hotblooded fools. But I also won't be seen as disloyal to my State."

Uncle Carter stood and began to pace in front of the fire; I sank behind the wings of my chair. "For better or worse, my situation is not suspect. I have daughters named Virginia and Georgia, a wife who is thoroughly Southern, and I'm not squeamish about slavery. I can be a Unionist without suspicion falling on me."

My uncle's voice took on a pleading note. "Lan, there's odd things being said about you already."

Papa got up and stood before the fire. I continued to lurk behind the chair wings and turned a page, in case he looked my way.

Carter continued: "Let me do the family arguing for now."

"You and Winston surely do agree." Papa sighed. "I'll keep my mouth shut. I know you mean the best."

"Thanks, Brother." Carter's voice was full of relief. "I have another favor to ask," he added. And, to my delight, he launched into the mystery Liza and I had puzzled over.

"Have you noticed Virginia's new maid?"

"Lord help us, yes! Who could ignore that girl?" Papa settled into his chair again.

"Precisely my problem," Uncle Carter replied.

"Where did she come from?" Papa asked.

"Remember Monty? We went to college together, but he lived in New Orleans after graduation, before coming back to Richmond. I still see him frequently."

"Adam Montcure? Surely. He visited for a couple of hunt seasons. What does he have to do with this girl?"

"I suspect he's her father. Not that he said so. But, I know he brought a baby home to Richmond when he returned from New Orleans. Later, he married and left the child at his mother's. Old Mrs. Adelaide Montcure died recently, and Monty took the girl into his own home."

A thrill ran through me. Fornication! A love child! I now knew about these things. I tingled with excitement.

I sneaked a glance at my father's disapproving face, as my uncle turned argumentative. "Well, look, his situation is really awkward! His wife took against her, and . . . well . . . I thought I'd help the fellow out. I had no idea I was taking on Helen of Troy!"

Helen of Troy. The most beautiful woman. How romantic! I squirmed deeper into the chair seat.

He began a rush of argument. "I can't let that girl out on the streets of Richmond, even on a simple errand. Twice already Virginia's complained about men accosting them on the side-walk when her maid was with her. Never a problem before. And my Dabney's at a susceptible age. You've got only girls, women, and little boys here, except for Horace, who's trustworthy. Rebecca'd be safe."

I held my breath. *Oh, please, Papa, let us keep her!*

What a wonderful moment! I thought to see my promise fulfilled with no action on my part at all. Uncle Carter and Papa would save Rebecca without my lifting a finger.

Now I knew of her Tragic Past, as well as her intolerable pre-sent. Unlike Mama, she had no loving husband to protect her when her father cast her off. She'd be happy here. I knew it.

"You forget," Papa answered. "Across that park is a school filled with other men's susceptible sons." But his voice sounded the way it did when he was about to give in to Mama's per-suasion.

"Would you trade me Daisy?" Uncle Carter asked. "Rebecca

could take her place helping Sapphire, and Virginia would still have a young servant."

My whole body tingled with horror, and a croak escaped me, but fortunately Papa was too upset to notice. "You're daft. Sapphire's lost her husband and sons; she's not losing Daisy."

"Be reasonable!" Carter said. "I can't go home to Emma and say I've *given* a servant away. Daisy would love Richmond; it's full of young servants. And she'd be back to visit her ma."

"No."

In part, I relaxed. Papa would never agree. But now my promise came back to haunt me. I would have to plan a rescue for Rebecca, if my uncle wouldn't voluntarily leave her with us.

There was a several-second pause, then Papa said, "If Rebecca comes with papers of manumission, she may stay until my wife's nieces go North. They'd place her through Meeting."

"I can't afford to give her away," Carter said. His chair scraped as he rose. They damped the fire in irritated silence, and left without a glance toward my end of the room.

In Which We
Have a Ball

NEXT morning the students turned their dining hall back into the ballroom it was intended to be. Larger boys removed the tables. Smaller boys lined chairs along the walls. There, chaperones, Wallflowers, even my sisters for an hour, would watch the dancing.

Horace, with Toby and Josh, collected cartfuls of holly and Virginia creeper. The students climbed ladders to hang greenery over doorways and window frames, behind mirrors and pictures, and twisted ropes of it around and down the staircase banisters.

Ruby and Pearl waxed floors, and Horace gave them a hard buffing. The branched chandeliers were lowered, and Liza, Isabel, and I rooted wax candles in several hundred holders, before they were pulled ceiling-ward. Oil lamps might light side rooms, but Mama insisted on candlelight in the ballroom.

The Jenkins ladies toiled in their kitchen, and Sapphire and Mama were equally busy in ours. Pepper-cured ham boiled in the baby-bath on the stove for hours, filling the air with grease-laden steam. A great-cake sat ready to go into the old brick oven in the Academy kitchen, to cook overnight once the coals were raked out. The weather was cool enough to preserve rich cream sauce over sponge cake, so the charlottes were stored on the porch, sheltered under sheet-tents to keep children from sampling.

The oyster man was due in the morning, when Horace would unlid the icehouse and chip one pile of ice to lay the half shells on, and a second pile for making ice cream. Toby and Josh had the tiresome duty of cranking the machine, but the result was a treat we waited for from July Fourth until December.

It was very nearly the same as any other Christmas.

———◆———

ON the morning of the Ball, Virginia burst into my room, dragging Rebecca. "Look at me!" she wailed. One side of her face was swollen.

She felt fine, but she was furious. Much as I disliked her, I couldn't help but feel some pity. She had been as excited over her first Ball as Liza.

The thought of Liza gave me pause.

The adults would put Virginia to bed, and make an end of it.

And Liza might blame me if I let that happen. I'd crossed my heart and promised to treat Virginia well. I had to decide *something*. Now. Before my sisters woke.

"Let's get out of sight," I said. "We'll go to Liza's till we figure what to do." I glanced at Rebecca, who smiled. "Rebecca must come, too."

My parents, Sapphire and her sisters, and the Jenkins women were preoccupied with slicing ham and smoked turkey, pressing linen, transporting food from our kitchen to the Academy, setting up punch bowls, and other such problems.

I announced that Virginia and I would be at Liza's. We grabbed breakfast from the sideboard. Toby had been dispatched to borrow Mrs. Wright's linen cloths, candlesticks, and punch ladle, so we hitched a ride. Virginia played martyr in the old cart, but I said we could return if she wished. She did not wish.

Liza was delighted to see us and was not the least put off by the mumps. "Oh, Win and I had them that summer we visited Aunt Katherine in Flat Rock," she said. "Mumps was nothing much." She turned to me. "You haven't had it?"

I shook my head. "Nor Rebecca, either."

Liza shrugged. "You're exposed already, but you can't come down with it till after Christmas, so don't worry." She patted Virginia's swollen jaw. "You'll be fine. In fact, I have an idea already. What fun! Mama has pictures of European royalty, from the time she was presented to the Queen. You must see them!" Liza ran to her mother's desk, pulled out a drawer and extracted an album.

"One of the ladies, I forget her name, has an elegant style, and a tulle scarf wrapped charmingly around her neck. Mama says she was whispered to have a goiter, which is much more disfiguring than mumps, but you'd never guess."

We crowded eagerly around, as Liza showed off the most glamorous moment of her mother's past. There, in a yellowing newspaper sketch, was a willowy lady in full court dress with a hairdo dressed in flowers and tulle. The flowers had been placed to emphasize the lady's eyes and hair, and the fine silk netting floated glamorously around jaw and neck, betraying no unsightly lump.

"We have tulle, from those dresses Mama gave us for our Christmas project," said Liza. She bounced on her toes with excitement. "And I'll sneak silk flowers from our summer bonnets. Mama will forgive us when she sees how we look. We'll outshine the other girls, never fear!"

Rebecca regarded the picture with the eyes of a true artist, and she was, indeed, good with hair. A genius.

By the time we rode back with Mr. Wright's coachman, carrying Liza's gown reverently packed in tissue, we all wore creations Mrs. Wright had agreed were suitable and becoming. Since Virginia had passed her close inspection, we were certain the distracted adults of the Big House would notice nothing.

Atha was indifferent toward the Ball, but Sophie assisted our preparations. "Your rose silk looks new with that elegant hairstyle," she whispered. Kind Sophie! The other girls were tricked out in more elaborate gowns.

I retrieved my locket from Mama's casket, and watched Virginia's eyes narrow. "That should be mine," she muttered to Liza, who cut her eyes toward me as she muttered, "Hush."

It is a sad truth—I flaunted that bauble. But, so it was.

"Ah!" said Sophie. "Thee's sure to be Belles!"

"Come watch us, at least," I begged.

She shook her head. "It would upset Atha, you know." She leaned toward me and whispered, "I'm sure she promised our mother to keep me from misdeeds. She would have to report such a failure. Then, too," she added, as she wrinkled her nose in amusement, "it would hurt my vanity to attend without a Ball gown—and to sit aside when the music called." She waved us off and returned to Olympus to spend the evening in more Quakerly pursuits.

We were successes. My card was full, as the students flocked to reserve dances. On the two occasions when I feared to be partnerless, Win appeared to escort me to the punch bowl.

Flirting was easiest with him, though I practiced on other partners, too. My dancing lessons had been painful, but the same steps were delightful with a young man as partner. I was tickled when Papa—who, as host, danced with every female who ventured onto the floor—complimented me as if I were a grown lady.

Both the Wrights were wonderfully coordinated, so their brother-sister waltz was a glory to behold. My parents considered the waltz rather too racy for young girls, but I'd learned it anyway, from Liza, at her house. "Poo!" she'd said. "*Everybody* waltzes now. You mustn't be a dowd."

So, scared but determined, I accepted a waltz with Win. I'd learned how to begin, but Win made a magic carpet of a dance floor. The whirl was intoxicating, and the warmth of Win's hands—one just behind my waist, pulling me close, and the other holding my own gloved fingers—had the thrill of the forbidden.

We hardly spoke, and I was breathless when the dance ended. For a moment, his hand stayed at my waist, and he pressed me toward the door to the verandah.

Virginia, towing Susan Stewart, blocked the exit and handed me my shawl. "You'll catch your death, Cousin Dear, if you go out like that," she said.

Win bowed handsomely to her. "I believe I signed your card for the next dance, Miss Chamberlyn," he said, and his hand slipped from my waist. "Shall we all take the air before the music starts again?"

I was both disappointed and relieved, as the four of us walked out together. I had thought of a kiss, perhaps, as Liza assured me it was delightful and one could always pretend to be shocked. "After all," she said, "it's the boy who must take the blame. No one will think you are *fast*. Everyone knows how boys are."

Something warned me, though, that perhaps Liza's advice had not taken into account the melting feeling from that masterful hand taking the lead, and the dizziness of the whirl. Did I like feeling I'd lost control? That what happened was not my fault? I wasn't sure.

Sixteen

In Which the Mumps
Complicate Life

WHEN the adults discovered next morning that Virginia had the mumps, she burst into tears and vowed I'd wheedled her into attending the dance.

She was now quite sick, with a fever and with both sides of her jaw swollen and painful. So I took the blame. I couldn't explain about my promise to Liza. Uncle Carter might easily cancel her Richmond visit. Besides, I'm not a tattler.

I stood before the fireplace in our library, as Papa and Uncle Carter sat in judgment in the chairs that flanked the hearth. "I'm sorry, Papa. We didn't think . . ."

"You are too old not to think, Evvy." Papa was solemn. He sighed. "If you don't use good sense, what can punishment do? Waywardness may be cured; stupidity is hard to remedy."

"We didn't mean—"

"Evelyn, it is certain that some of Virginia's dancing partners will pass the disease along. This Academy will be responsible for disrupting who knows how many households and communities before the illness runs its course."

Papa frowned and drummed his fingers on the chair's arm.

"This may delay the new semester. Some boys may not return until spring—or not at all. What you meant is irrelevant."

"I must leave Virginia here," Uncle Carter joined in. "I'll have to retrieve her in the worst weather of the year."

"Yes, Sir," I whispered, with my eyes on the floor.

"You may leave, Evelyn," said my father. I blinked back tears as I walked toward the door.

"I assume Rebecca may remain as long as Virginia's here?" My uncle's voice was extraordinarily polite. Even if I hadn't overheard him earlier, I'd have known something was strange. I slowed my step; the need to know gripped me.

"Naturally," Papa said. "We can discuss further when you return."

I walked into the hall, but left the door ajar and stood quietly, just out of sight.

Papa's voice rose, hard and angry. "But, Carter, persuade Monty before you come back. The girl's own father could hardly, in decency, refuse to free the child."

"Watch yourself, Landon," my uncle warned. "Monty's done nothing worse than our own father. You own slaves yourself. We're decent men; we just don't agree with you."

The scraping of my uncle's chair alarmed me, and I scuttled down the corridor before he burst through the door and strode down the hall. Curiosity sent me to peep around the corner, as he snatched his greatcoat from the hall tree and headed to the stables.

So he was gone, and I was stuck with Virginia. To add to that, Papa had forbidden holiday visiting, even Church, to avoid further spread of mumps. Instead of attending the holiday frivolities of the neighborhood, we were confined to home.

A week later, Isabel, Annalee, and Baby Beatrice were swollen, but not much affected.

Then Papa became dangerously ill. The disease that had hardly seemed worth the worry became sinister. I'd thought of mumps as a child's disease. Almost a joke. And for the little girls it was. They looked silly, but were still hard to keep in bed, and likely to be playing about barefooted any time we left them unattended.

But Papa's fever ran high and he was often incoherent. He couldn't eat, and the liquids Sapphire insisted he must have were hard to force down him.

Mama and Sapphire took turns in Papa's room, while Pearl and Ruby nursed the girls, and Rebecca and I tended Virginia. We'd already been so exposed that caution seemed unnecessary. Mama ordered my cousins, who'd never had mumps, to stay in Olympus. Sapphire and I handed in meals from the porch.

"No sense in you two exposing yourselves," Sapphire protested when Atha and Sophie begged to take a turn at nursing. "Just make trouble for us later. Now, I'm not taking nonsense from you; this mumps is mean on men, but it's hard on any full-grown person. When Miss Felicity and me need something, Toby and Josh'll help; they should get those mumps while they're little."

So Atha and Sophie lived isolated, except when Mr. Rawley stopped by to discuss the decline and fall of Rome.

Daisy, Joycelyn, and Nelly puffed up the same day. Then Rebecca swelled, and joined Daisy in the Blue Room, where we could tend them more easily than in quarters. This bumped the now-better Virginia to my bed.

It sounds hectic, but mostly it was boring, filled with whining children and increasingly bad weather. Sleet mixed with snow made even a walk outdoors impossible.

Anxiety rose as Papa's illness peaked. I'd never seen Papa suffer with more than a cough, but now my mother and Sapphire were worrying as if he were sick enough to die. And it would be my fault, for if he hadn't danced with Virginia, he might not have been sick at all. I had only recently begun to see Mama as mortal; now Papa was frail, too.

Eventually, Papa began to recover, and an irritable mood seized us all. Virginia flounced like a Tragedy Queen, moaning over being stuck in the country, and angry to have no servant. Even she hadn't the nerve to order Sapphire and her sisters around, and Daisy and Rebecca were bedridden.

They were less sick than they acted, however. They were delighted with each other's company, thrilled to escape chores, and happy to be waited on. By me. The still-well one.

I grumbled to Ruby, who went to check for herself when merriment issued from the supposed sickroom. Ruby loved a good laugh, and, the next thing I knew, she'd settled right in to enjoy their company, leaving me simmering in the hall.

I was in a mood to feel petulant and put-upon, and I suspected I was the butt of some joke. I marched down the hall to embarrass them, but Ruby had a loud voice, and soon I could hear she was only describing my father's looks and teasing the girls about their own lumpy faces.

Ruby's voice turned sober. "I'm joking, and Marse Landon looks a hoot, but he's been awful sick." She lowered her voice, and I moved toward the door.

"Now, Sapphire says that's not all to the bad. Marse can't give Miss Felicity more babies. On the other hand, unless the baby Sapphire suspicions Missus is carrying now is a boy, the plantation's bound go to young Marse Dabney. Won't be more chances."

"Ugh. He's a horrid young man," said Rebecca.

"You mean Marse Landon can't have more children?" asked Daisy. "From *mumps*?"

I was as startled as Daisy, and I thought I'd better keep listening.

"My mama and grandmama thought so, and Sapphire, too, so I believe it," Ruby said. "If I do say so myself, I have smart relatives. Mumps don't hurt little boys much, but grown men get in-fer-tile."

"Infertile?" asked Daisy. "Where did you learn that?"

"I asked Miss Atha what to call not being able to have babies, and she said 'in-fer-tile,' " Ruby answered. "She gives me words all the time. It's what she calls 'vo-cab-u-lary.' "

"Wish that infertile thing would happen to that Dabney," said Rebecca. "He bothers me all the time back in Richmond. He spies on me. Any time I'm alone, even for a minute, he's there all of a sudden. He tries to touch me, asks me to meet him somewhere. I'm afraid to walk even to the outhouse without another girl along." Her voice suddenly rose again with hope. "Maybe this mumps will take care of him?"

I froze. The meaning of *bothers* was only too clear to me, as I recalled the scene at my schoolhouse. Dabney bothering and Virginia bossing. Rebecca's life was worse than I'd thought.

Ruby sounded cheerful as she gave advice: "Rebecca, Honey, mumps don't take away the urge, just the babies. You still got to be careful."

Daisy began telling her tale of Dabney's attack, a story I knew only too well. I crept away to consider Ruby's words.

Rebecca was glamorous. Beyond that, she'd turned out to be a genuinely nice person. Everyone liked her.

Dabney, on the other hand, was not nice. I did not doubt

that he'd stalk Rebecca until he caught her alone, if she returned to Richmond.

Yet my world supported him, not her.

And not me. Not the person I really was, nor what I truly believed.

Suddenly, unaccountably, my Inner Light picked this moment to flare. The lot of women *was not fair,* and no amount of flirtation and silk dresses and compliments could hide that.

My Cause had grabbed me, as the Cause of slavery had seized others. I didn't even know what name to put on it. My Cause, I mean. Or how to do anything to further it.

The only thing I knew how to do was teach. Could that be a start? Most girls got very little schooling. Without knowledge, what tools would they have for proving they could think and act as well as boys? But my heart sank as I thought of the trouble ahead. That I was obliged to do something was clear. But everyone I knew—not just the reverend lecturer, but the Wrights, the Stewarts, my own parents, even Sapphire, even Atha—would think me crazy to have such thoughts. I hadn't any desire to play the martyr.

An *Inner Light* had sounded so noble. Who would expect a pesky misery that could only lead to hard work and a reputation for insanity?

Seventeen

In Which I Confide in My Cousins

AFTER a night of fitful sleep, I decided to escape to Olympus, whether I carried the plague or not. I promised myself I'd sit across the room, to be safe. However, I'd really decided I must be, for some unknown reason, immune to mumps.

I bundled up and plunged through sleet for the short distance between the new and old kitchens.

Red mud slipped under me and oozed over my soles. I stomped onto the porch, swiped my shoes on the mat, and burst into the schoolroom.

Atha and Mr. Rawley were standing close to each other, staring at me. Sophie was nowhere in sight.

"Oh," I said.

"I was just leaving," said Mr. Rawley.

"Please, don't leave on account of me," I replied.

"Not at all," he said, turning toward Atha. "I must be off. I'm delighted that you found volume three so excellent." He grabbed his coat from the desk, struggled into the sleeves, wrapped a scarf, donned the hat resting on the dictionary, and bumped me in his dash for the door. "G'bye," he said, nodding, and was gone.

"Where's Sophie?" I asked.

"Here!" Sophie bounced down the stairs. "Come in! We're perishing for company. Let's make tea and hear all the gossip from the infirmary." She dipped some water from the rain barrel, poured it into a pan, set it on the stovetop, and produced a teapot.

"Go set the table," said Atha. "I'll bring the pot up when it's brewed." The awkward moment passed, and I followed Sophie to the second floor.

"How does thee like my new apron-dress?" Sophie twirled to demonstrate. "Mama sent us fabric, and Atha and I have been sewing to pass time till school starts again."

"I like it; you've improved Mama's pattern. And it looks so comfortable. I . . . fear Mama will need some, too—she . . . came down this morning in her Chinese jacket," I blurted. "That means she's increasing." I began to cry.

"Well, but how delightful," said Sophie. "Why is thee upset?"

"Mama shouldn't have more babies," I said.

"Why so?" asked Atha, walking in with the teapot. "Many women have a dozen, and she's never lost an infant."

"Sapphire says so, and she knows about these things. . . ."

"Did Sapphire tell thee that?" asked Sophie.

"No." Reluctantly I admitted, "Before you all came, I was worried, and asked Daisy. She says her mammy warned Mama before Annalee and Papa before Beatrice."

Atha and Sophie became quite still for a moment. Then, "I understand she's an excellent midwife," said Atha, pouring tea as she spoke. Her hand shook, and tea landed in my saucer. I knew she was nervous, despite her brave words.

"There is nothing we can do, Sister. Thee knows it is right for married couples to be fruitful." Sophie put her saucer on the table with a firm *click*. "Our being here helps."

"You will stay till the baby comes, won't you?" I begged.

"Of course." Sophie patted my hand. "Just think, another darling baby! I do hope for a girl, though your parents may want a son, after six daughters."

"It's not just a matter of 'want,' " I replied. "Daisy says Grandfather Justin's Will left the plantation to Papa only for his life, and then to his son. If he has none, Dabney gets it. If this baby isn't a boy, what would Mama do if Papa died?"

Atha sat straight and sniffed before speaking. "It seems to me, Daisy has entirely too much to say about our aunt and uncle."

Sophie smiled at Atha and arched her brows. "Remember? Aunt told Mama that the Negro folk know more about the family they work for than the family itself. I suspect Sapphire knows everything, as her mammy did before her, and her grandmammy before that." She looked serious as she added, "Still, Evvy dearest, our own mama dislikes idle chat with our hired girls."

Atha relaxed, and poured a cup of tea for herself. "Our upbringing has been so different, I tend to forget . . ." Her voice trailed off, as she sipped.

"Forget what?" I asked.

"Forget how complicated other peoples' ways are. I came expecting anger and resentment, even hatred, between slaves and owners. But what I've seen has been respect and love. Both ways. What is it I don't see?"

Atha stared into my face, and asked, "Evelyn, do you never wonder what's behind Sapphire's dignity? Behind Ruby's joking and Pearl's calm?" She shook her head. "I can't believe these able women passively accept bondage."

"I asked Sapphire if she hated Great-aunt Jane, and she said she did, for a time, but not since she joined the Railroad. She doesn't feel passive, I reckon."

I stared back at Atha. "She loves Mama. I know she does. And Mama loves her. And Daisy said she didn't hold anything against me. They want to be here. If they didn't, they could leave. Papa offered to free them, soon as he inherited them."

Atha shook her head again and said, "I've seen so little of other households. Dinner with the Wrights and Williamses, tea with the Stewart ladies. Yet, I think there's a . . . difference. Other homes don't somehow feel as . . . comfortable." She frowned in puzzlement. "Am I right?"

"It may be you are." I tried to think. There were things. . . . The girls I knew—Liza or Susan—were pleasant to servants, but perhaps not polite? I gave it up. My cousins, for all their sympathy, had reduced my anger at the fate of females, both slave and not, to servants' gossip, and turned the discussion back to slavery.

But it was *women* who bore the danger of babies; *women* who became poor if widowed; *women* who got disinherited; *women* who feared attack. Slavery wasn't right—but this wasn't right, either. I tried again.

"What if Mama dies? If the new baby's a girl? If Papa should die before Mama? Why should boys be better than girls?" I began to cry again.

"Why, Evvy, you take on so!" Atha pulled her chair near mine and put an arm around my shoulders. "On our side of the family, girls are best! Mama says if we marry, pray for girls, and Grandma recites:

> 'A son is a son till he gets him a wife,
> But a daughter's a daughter the whole of her life.' "

"Here." Sophie pulled a fresh kerchief from her sleeve and pushed it into my hand, rattling off comforting thoughts.

"Your papa won't die for many, many years. By then, he'll

have tucked money aside for your mama. Maybe buy a nice little house in Richmond to rent till she needs it. Our mama would never let her sister want, you know that. And once you girls marry, you'll have homes for your mama if she needs help. And even if this baby's a girl, the next may be a boy."

I let the tears flow and soaked up the sympathy. But part of me was weeping for *me,* not Mama.

I considered telling them Papa was infertile now, but Atha disapproved of servants' gossip; even Sophie did. Telling them what Daisy had outright told me was hard enough. To admit I'd eavesdropped on Ruby seemed impossible. And since Ruby had learned *infertile* from Atha, there was no hope of hiding the source of the information.

Though Sophie and Atha were good, and I loved them, confession hadn't relieved me. That Inner Light kept nudging me, insisting women's lives were unfair and I had a duty to *do* something. Save Mama, protect Rebecca, defeat Dabney.

But what could I do?

The answer appeared to be: nothing.

In Which I Begin
to Discover
the Real Great-aunt Jane

IN FEBRUARY, the girls flocked back to classes, to the joy of my very bored cousins. The Academy, though, started slowly; many students were, as Papa had predicted, recovering from mumps.

Uncle Carter wrote he'd be delayed in retrieving Virginia. She wept, but Papa was elated. "He's attending the Peace Conference in Washington. Excellent! We Unionists have a chance to hold the country together." He patted Virginia. "Be proud your papa may save us from war." He ignored her pout.

Now I contracted mumps—after everyone else was well. Virginia went back to the Blue Room with Rebecca, who was safe while my cousin stayed. Things could be worse.

At first I was miserable, but after two weeks my aching jowls slimmed toward normal. Recuperating in bed, I was bored. I decided to write Aunt Honor. My hope was she'd insist her daughters stay longer if she knew how much we needed them.

I sat bundled up before Great-aunt Jane's desk, sharpening pens, testing them on scratch sheets, and fooling with drawers, pigeonholes, and ornamental knobs as I composed in my head.

One drawer pulled out completely and was shorter than its counterpart on the facing side of the desk. I explored this, reaching into the empty slot, where I hit a sort of lever. The whole block of pigeonholes and drawers jumped. As I pulled my hand out, the section moved with a hinged motion.

A slice of black appeared on the right side of the moving portion of the desk. I grabbed an edge and pulled gently. The entire block swung out, hitting the inkwell, bumping it toward my lap. I placed it on the floor, and pulled further.

What had seemed a thin ornamental skirt below the foldout writing surface was actually a disguise for a cavity that reached from the writing surface to the floor. It was eight inches from front to back, and the width of the desk—some forty inches.

There was no doubt about it. A secret compartment! From beating at double-time, my heart slowed to a standstill.

I peered inside. Notebooks filled it; they were similar in size, and simply thrust in, with their bindings facing up.

I removed them. Each front binder had an inscription: *Private Journal of Miss Jane Chamberlyn,* followed by a beginning and ending date. A glance into a random book confirmed that the entry on page one was, indeed, the first date on the binder, and the last entry coincided with the second date.

I read a few pages, but they were fairly ordinary. My father's tenth birthday recorded. A colt born out of Lucky Lady by Cyclone. Molly had cured several fieldhands of some disease. Brother Justin had left for Richmond.

I carried the notebooks to the bed and sorted them by year. Soon, the entire period of the writing was laid in order. The first was dated when my father was nearly as young as Beatrice, the final one began shortly before my own birth—and thus only a few months before Jane's death. Years of secrets!

I was actually panting, as if I'd run flights of stairs instead of flights of fancy. I forced myself to choose one—the final book, since my birth was surely in it. I threw a quilt over the rest, in case anyone visited unexpectedly.

In the window seat I flipped to my birthdate. The exact date was skipped, but the next entry fascinated me.

> *Five days since, Felicity was delivered of a girl, Evelyn. Sapphire's a competent midwife, and her sisters did well by her three days later. She had a girl, too. Odd, isn't it, Justin? Twins, almost. You should be here to share the jest.*
>
> *My Dear, at last we have another real Chamberlyn. Much as we adored your sons, they were always too like their mother. Bland. A bit too virtuous. This child is your mirror (and mine). Her eyes are blue, as with all infants, but they will turn, I think. She's more me than you. And so like us, Brother—as young Dabney is not.*
>
> *Justin, how could you cheat me and Landon, too? I did as promised by Carter, but you broke your solemn word. The Hall was to have been Landon's, free and clear. Now I see the worst of it—we have a true Chamberlyn, but a girl. Yet, Emma's brat may inherit our homeplace. I cannot condone that.*

I felt smug, knowing I was a "true Chamberlyn." A surge of affection ran through me for this old lady. I felt something else, too—I was *entitled* to inherit. *I* was the true Chamberlyn, the legitimate heir. I had more right than Dabney, "Emma's brat." A Will that "cheated" could not, after all, be the sacred thing Papa had said it was.

I skimmed to the end of the booklet. Entries covered small news. Many addressed Justin; several scolded about the terms of his Will. The elegant handwriting became a scrawl, then, painful printing. "No more. Good-bye journal, my constant friend." This, I concluded, marked the stroke of apoplexy I knew had triggered a collapse and soon ended her life.

The rest of my illness was delightful. I spent hours in the window seat, impatient of visitors.

I was fascinated by the naughty boy who'd grown into my now-starchy father, along with his brother, and their crony Winston. Sapphire was already curing sick animals, and Ruby had to be disciplined for practical jokes. Everyone quite doted on Baby Pearl, much as we now did on Beatrice. Jane had supported Uncle Carter's choice of the College of New Jersey at Princeton over Harvard; she'd fought with Justin when my father stayed North to teach in Paul and Honor's school. About my mother, she remarked: "So smart, so beautiful, so sweet natured. It ain't natural."

The most startling notebook was the first, though I describe it last. Here, Jane told of coming home from the Grand Tour she'd taken to give Justin's wife, her young sister-in-law Letitia, "a chance to rule her own home."

However, Jane had been thrilled at the news of Letitia's death from childbed fever after Uncle Carter's birth. "I wished her no ill," she claimed. And she blamed Justin's stupidity in hiring a medical doctor (man-midwife, she termed him) to attend the birth, instead of trusting Molly, Sapphire's competent and experienced grandmother. Personally, Jane rejoiced. She could go home again and be mistress of the plantation.

I could never have obeyed a Husband. Nor could I have lived an Old Maid in another woman's house. Where Justin is concerned, I have, Thank God, NO Duty of Obedience. He rather obeys me, than I obey him.

I laughed out loud, and smothered the sound with my hand, lest anyone passing my door wonder what amused me on my sickbed. *So much,* I thought, *for Papa's theory that Jane sacrificed herself for her brother and his sons.*

She'd rushed back to Virginia on the first ship she could find. She feared that Justin might remarry in haste, so she bid a hasty adieu to someone discussed only as "the Marquis."

I shall never mention him, for although his Wife cared not a whit (Frenchwomen seem generally to favor Other Men over their Husbands) I do not think Virginia Society would approve.

I giggled again, as I imagined Papa reading this. *I'll never show it to him, though,* I thought. No good could come of it— and I felt a loyalty to both that seemed to demand silence.

In Which I Uncover
Secrets That Are
Not Amusing

So far, I had thoroughly enjoyed every one of Jane's confidences. Now an affair with far more serious consequences revealed itself. As I kept reading, it dawned on me what Grandfather Justin had done to resemble Uncle Carter's friend Monty.

Again, Jane stated that Heaven favored her plans. Her brother was away in Charleston when she arrived home from Europe, and she'd used this opportunity to set things aright. One important entry concerned Sapphire's mother and grandmother.

When Jane left for her Grand Tour, she congratulated herself on leaving the household in good working order. Old Molly had been moved into the Big House to be housekeeper until Letitia's first baby's arrival, which was expected within a year or so. Molly would then move into the nursery in the position of mammy to the baby. Molly's daughter Tessa would be cook, physically demanding work better suited to a young woman.

Yet, on Jane's unexpected return, three years later she found Molly was back in the kitchen, while Tessa had the easier job of nursemaid to the two little boys and lived in the Big House. That wasn't all. Her journal recorded another discovery:

*A blue-eyed Infant Darky shared the Nursery with Lan-
don and Carter. Those Eyes were unmistakably J's. That
bright coloration. Molly confirmed the truth, and hinted
that Tessa and Samson, over at Wright's Rest, "favored"
each other.*

Those Eyes were unmistakably J's. The phrase shook me. I
felt chilled. I grabbed a quilt and wrapped it round me. Jane, I realized, had a habit of taking advantage of another's absence.

*I hastened to Wright's Rest—twisted Winston's arm until
he sold me Samson. The man cost a Pretty Penny, but
was worth it. I arranged a Real Marriage, which perhaps
was excessive, but by the time J. returned, all was fait ac-
compli. Tessa was in cook's quarters over the kitchen
with her New Husband and her Baby, and her Mother
was reinstated in the Nursery with my nephews. They
are, thank Heaven, young enough to forget the Whole Incident.*

I remembered Samson as a kind old man who told us chil-
dren tall tales. I returned to the puzzle of the "blue-eyed Infant
Darky." That Justin's eyes were remarkable showed in his picture.
Who could this "darky" be? I read on.

*I told J. I would not preside over an Immoral Household,
and if he ever indulged himself again, I should take the
boys to the Richmond house and raise them alone, in
Pure Surroundings. He gave me no Backtalk. Indeed, I
suspect he was relieved to have his problem solved with
so little inconvenience. Ah! These men!*

Upon reading this, I sat for a solid hour in the window seat, knees to chin, and stared out the window, pondering.

Sapphire was the one of Tessa's children with blue eyes. Now that I considered this, yes, her eyes had that bright blue sparkle, though her darker skin set them off differently.

My *grandfather*, it appeared, was Sapphire's *father*.

But then I thought, if Sapphire were Grandfather Justin's daughter, she'd be Papa's half sister—and my aunt. Daisy was my cousin. They *were* my family. I could hardly believe it.

I thought of Sapphire's laughter as she said I favored Old Jane "awful much." Could "true Chamberlyns" be counted among God's elect? I doubted it. For a moment, I had a vision of Isabel flapping around Heaven with Mama while I rolled on the brimstone with Great-aunt Jane and Grandpa Justin.

This was what Uncle had meant when he said Rebecca's father was no worse than old Justin. *This* was the joke Jane saw behind my almost-birthday with Daisy: Justin had become a grandfather to "almost-twin" granddaughters through his son Landon and his daughter Sapphire.

For perhaps half an hour I tried to find a mistake. But, no. My jaws ached, only partly from mumps. I was gritting my teeth.

Sapphire had said that hate was destructive—but only to the hater, not the hated. Justin was dead and gone. I made an effort to refuse to hate him. And, many books later, I was glad to find reason to like him: Justin had defied his sister, not only about Papa's inheritance, but on another point as well. And this provision was one I could applaud. *He had freed Sapphire despite Jane's opposition.*

Jane had instructed him, as she wrote in her journal:

The matter is over and done. There is no sense
publishing his Error to the World by freeing one blue-
eyed Child, leaving the rest of her Family in Service.

Jane had expected her brother to write his Will as she'd dictated. Nevertheless, she'd rummaged through her brother's desk after his death and read his Will before the attorney saw it. She was furious to find he'd defied her wishes in two ways.

First, that Justin had limited Landon's inheritance to a mere "life estate," with the property fully inherited only at the grandchild generation: by Carter's son, if Landon had no boys.

He claimed this would prevent any Sale of Plantation
Properties during Landon's lifetime, and would Preserve
the Chamberlyn line for at least two more generations,
perhaps forever. Ha! Such Vanity! As if a Family can
only be preserved by Persons sporting Male Equipment!

I joined Aunt Jane's anger—but soon found myself in total disagreement with her.

At Sapphire's birth, Justin had written a manumission, providing freedom for "the child born this day to my slave Tessa." At his death, he'd expected his lawyer to find the manumission with his Will. But Jane had taken her revenge. "Naught can I do about the life estate," she lamented.

I have, however, disposed of the manumission. The Will
does not, by its own terms, free Sapphire, and I will not
permit Justin to play Fast and Loose with Landon's In
heritance. Sapphire and her offspring go to Lan's portion,
and I shall see to it. Felicity may have only Personal

Property to keep her from the Poor House, disinherited as
she is, Poor Dear.

I stared through the window to the rainy day, and then focused on a large drop making an erratic trail along the pane.
Odd, how a casual thing will linger in memory, linked to something completely different. I never watch a drop run without
feeling, again, the shock of how evil and virtue can mingle in
anyone, myself included.

Sapphire had said Miss Jane was sneaky to compensate for
"disabilities of age and sex." Well! I knew about those, though in
my case the age was very young, in her case very old.

Calling people "personal property" was natural to Jane, but
disturbing to me. I valued her regard for my mother, but her
notion that Mama might sell off Sapphire and her children was
unbelievable. At least Justin had freed his daughter at birth, and
he'd stood by that decision.

But, secretly. To avoid a fight with his sister he'd put off letting Sapphire know until he died. Coward! And then, of course,
he'd been outmaneuvered.

I glanced again at the journal. What did "disposed" mean?
Would Jane have burned the manumission?

I recalled a scrap glimmering from the dark bottom of the
secret hiding-hole, out of reach.

Isabel brought a candle with my supper; when she left, I
held it down the hole. Sure enough, something pale tannish-
white gleamed in a corner. Finally, I thought to tie a hatpin to
my mother's yardstick; once pierced, the object easily drew up
the side.

It proved to be vellum, written in a fine, firm hand, and was, indeed, the manumission, or "freedom paper," for the "girl-child born this day to my slave known as Tessa."

THAT night, Sapphire came to check me over, and pronounced me cured. I took a chance. "Is it true, Grandfather's Will claimed he'd freed you, Sapphire?"

"Who said so?"

I wasn't about to answer that. "Is it true?"

"Yes."

"What happened to the papers? Do you know?"

Sapphire shrugged. "Maybe he thought better of it. Maybe Miss Jane stole them. Maybe the lawyer did. Doesn't matter, because your papa offered to free us anyway."

"When, Sapphire?"

"When he inherited us, soon after Marse Justin died. He called me and my sisters in and told us about this group of men who send freed slaves to a country called Liberia, and he offered to free us and send us."

"Where's Liberia?"

"It's over in Africa, near where my grandmammy Molly came from." Sapphire bit her lip and paused. "We said no."

"Why did you say no?"

Sapphire looked me in the eye. "Life was good here, even better since your mama came and Marse Justin died. My sisters and I didn't want to leave our home, which by law we'd have to do. I figured Miss Jane would never free my Julius, nor would Marse Carter, when he inherited him, no matter what your pa did or said. Could I leave my Julius?"

She paused, looking for a response.

"No. Of course you couldn't."

"I couldn't leave him. My sisters couldn't leave me. After Julius was sold, I figured this is where he knew to find me when he got free." She shrugged slightly, sighed, and added, "Then . . . after . . . I had the Station. Couldn't desert that."

She stood and patted my shoulder. "You're fine, Honey. Church tomorrow, school Monday."

I was relieved. I didn't have to confess about the journals; Sapphire didn't want the paper anyway. I tucked it back among the notebooks and wrote that long-delayed letter to Aunt Honor. The words came easily this time, and the quill never blotted.

In Which the Bad Times
Begin in Earnest

SO ENDED February and the plague of mumps. March rains mucked the roads. Liza rode over, but fear of a mired vehicle kept the other girls away. Mud sucked off boots and dyed hems a permanent red.

Uncle Carter wrote that the Peace Conference had failed. He'd left Washington only hours before Lincoln's inauguration, after all hope was gone. Papa was deeply upset. He read portions of the letter aloud to us in the parlor, leaving out the cuss words I could see over his shoulder. His voice choked a bit over the final sentence:

> *Brother, the politicians won't let the South go without a fight. We will have War. It is only a question of how it starts.*

For a moment, we were silent. Then Virginia asked, "Uncle Landon, when will Papa come get me?"

"He says his law practice needs attention. He sends love and bids you make the most of your studies."

Virginia burst into tears and fled the room. "I want to go hoooome," she wailed. Mama and Sophie ran to soothe her.

———————

In April, the weather improved. Olympus's students returned, giving us relief from each other's company. Papa perked up; our State had not left the Union; no war had begun. "Perhaps Carter was too pessimistic," he said to my cousins, who gladly agreed.

It was now, in this season of hope, that the terrible times befell us. The first, and worst, happened on a crisp Sunday in early April, only days before Fort Sumter fell and war began.

Our baby, little Beatrice, burned to death.

My cousins had decided to take a walk instead of sitting silent in Meeting as they'd done all winter. They donned over-sized apron-dresses, packed a luncheon, then waved good-bye after breakfast.

Mama put the three youngest in the parlor to keep warm and clean as the rest of us scurried to dress for Church. "Take care to stay fresh, now," she said, as always, and hurried to put on her own finishing touches.

Virginia and I were getting our hair done by Rebecca, and Isabel was finishing off Nelly at their washstand. Joycelyn said afterward that she was reading aloud to Annalee, from *Improving Stories for Children,* which was permitted on Sunday. Nobody was watching Beatrice, now toddling in short petticoats and curious about everything. The fire must have attracted her.

The first we knew was Annalee shrieking, and the terrible sound of a wailing animal above that, and Joycelyn yelling "MamaPapaHelpComeHelp!" as the parlor door—closed to keep the room warm—banged onto the hall's wall to let Joycelyn's voice fill the house.

———————

We ran, everyone, without time to think, and Papa leapt down the stairs before us, four sets at a time, shoeless and shirtless.

I reached the parlor door to see him sweep up a small rug and wrap it around a moving torch, falling, rolling himself and the bundle on the floor.

"Get Sapphire," he ordered, and I fled the house, running out the kitchen door, my stockinged feet pounding through mud, my hands over my ears to shut the sound, gasping fresh air to rid my nose of the smell of burn.

I think Sapphire knew Beatrice could not be saved, yet she tried her best. Our mother seemed to shrivel as hours passed and she sat murmuring to the cocoon that was our baby.

Papa hovered helpless, his hands and forehead blistered, and his hair smelling of singe. Horace left for the doctor. Ruby and Pearl shooed us out to Ruby's cabin, away from the smell and the sound of Mama sobbing. Pearl kept saying "It was an *accident*," as my sisters wept and said, "If only I had . . ."

Virginia sat shuddering in a corner; Rebecca did as the older women bid—heated wash water, made tea, walked Joycelyn.

Annalee curled in my lap, sucked her thumb, whimpered, and finally slept. Toby helped me move her to a bed; my arms and legs had gone to sleep, and I could hardly move. I began wandering from cabin to house to cabin, unable to settle.

Daisy stayed by her mother's side, unwrapping bandages or measuring medicine as ordered. Dr. Williams came. He had no cure, but left laudanum for Mama to take when she could stomach it.

"I'll tell your minister and the ladies," he said to me in the hall. "Do you want Jethro to build a coffin?"

I nodded, unable to speak, horrified to be responsible for

such a decision. But the adults were closeted with Beatrice. I was the only one around to decide. Soon, Papa carried a limp Mama upstairs to bed, and Daisy told me Baby had "passed on."

My cousins returned in the minister's carriage. He'd found them walking homeward. They pulled the household together: Fires were rebuilt, prayers said, soup and bread served, children put to bed with an adult in the room.

The next two days were a blur of ladies and girls coming in shifts, bearing cake and fruit and boiled eggs and ham and biscuits, as if food could fill up the emptiness of a missing baby. A folding screen appeared in the parlor, and behind it was the box Jethro had built.

Mrs. Wright brought yards of black ribbon and braid. Pearl trimmed my sisters' white dresses with rows of braid on the hems and sleeves. The ribbon became fresh sashes. Liza owned a black dress, which she loaned me, making do herself with her gray silk.

Old Mrs. Stewart, who was hard of hearing, shouted, "What a turrible pity poor Felicity couldn't have the baby photographed. She won't have nothing in her album to remember by. And that Mr. Clark takes such sweet, natural poses, too." At least no one pressed us to kiss what remained of Beatrice; the coffin stayed lidded.

Uncle Carter arrived, alone, only minutes before the service at our Church; Winston Wright had telegraphed him and met his train. He sat behind our family, the ever-tearful Virginia clinging to him, and he leaned forward to put his hand on Papa's shoulder through most of the service. Later, at the graveside, too. Mama stood, braced by Papa's arm around her, and Uncle hovered behind, with his hand still on his brother.

Virginia had never seemed fond of the baby, but then I'd been more casual than doting myself. Remorse swept over me to think I'd taken Bea's sweet baby ways for granted, and I figured Virginia was shaken, too. I liked her better for crying.

But right at the door of the church she'd thrown herself on her father, screaming, "Take me away from here! I can't stand it!" He'd calmed her and made her sit beside him in the pew, but now I knew her tears were self-pity, not grief.

Beatrice had been a funny little thing, more engaging than Nelly or Annalee had been. But even more—somehow, the anchor. The bottom of the line of girls, as I was the top. There was a completeness that I'd taken for granted. Now it was broken.

Daisy nodded when I tried to explain. "Now you know," she said, not unsympathetically. "There's just no way, till it happens to you." She hugged my shoulders.

She drew me from the groups clustered around the grave or drifting toward carriages, and lowered her voice. "A train's coming through. Bad timing, what with your uncle here, but we can't stop it. The worst is, we've got to risk Rebecca on it."

Dazed, I closed my eyes and tried to understand. Train? The ache of missing Beatrice and the sad, white face of Mama made anything but this funeral unreal. I was suddenly furious with Daisy. "*Worst!* This is the worst!"

She held her ground. "For you, maybe. Other folks have hard times, too." She crossed her arms. "Mammy and I loved that baby." Her chin and voice trembled. "We did all we could."

I thought of Sapphire working over the tiny body, Daisy aiding her mother for hours. No one else but Mama had been able to. . . . I was ashamed. Daisy, like her mother, was usually right.

"Rebecca's got nobody but us. No family. And looking like

she does, she can't just take off. She needs a safe group. She figures Marse Carter will take her back to Richmond with Miss Virginia. So, now's the time."

We paced toward the carriages as a group moved near. Daisy put her arm around me, to bring me close for a whisper.

"Except Dan and Eli, we've never added to the train from hereabouts. And they left before the Quakers came."

"Why does that matter?"

"If folks start disappearing from one place, the hunters, they search there. And we've got Quakers. Everybody knows Quakers hate slavery. Where else would they look? We could all get in trouble. Lose the station, too."

Liza and Win were heading for us in a determined way. "I'll see what I can find out," I said, moving to meet my friends. "Don't do anything yet; there's a chance she'll be freed anyway. I'll let you know, soon as I hear what Uncle plans to do."

The assembled crowd filled the carriages and headed for our house. We'd had visitors for two days, but the entire neighborhood—much the same group invited to tea in November—united now, to eat the quantities of food and to condole.

Guests or not, didn't matter to Mama. I helped Sapphire put her to bed. For the rest of us, though, even Papa, the sociability forced the hours onward. As afternoon wore into evening, the men drifted into the library. When I paused by the door to listen, Papa's friends were using bourbon and politics to divert his mind and ease his misery.

Isabel and I and our cousins dispensed hospitality to the ladies in the parlor. Our visitors came armed with improving stories and poetry on the subject of dying children. One after another read about the Little Angel who was sent to "win our hearts from pleasures here below" and to "beckon us to meet again in Heaven."

Then Annalee stamped her foot and said, "But I don't want to wait for Heaven! Why didn't God keep Baby Beatrice safe here with us, if He's so good?" Isabel marched her to the kitchen, but I slipped in after, with a hug and a candy.

Mrs. Wright and Liza stayed in Mama's bedroom, contrary to their sociable natures. But—they'd once lost a baby, too. When I tiptoed in, I'd find them giving Mama a sip of tea, or bathing her forehead in rosewater, or merely filling the hollow silence with the squeak of rocking chairs.

Eventually everybody cleared out except Uncle Carter and Mr. Wright. I was glad they were there. Papa needed them.

Twenty-one

In Which I
Acquire a Slave

THE LADIES had carted off their empty platters, pots, and bowls. Little was left for Ruby and Pearl to clear. Our cousins put the children to bed, then went to Olympus. Virginia tried clinging to her father, who dismissed her to her own room, Rebecca trailing.

I'd not forgotten my promise to Daisy, but there'd been swarms of people ever since. Now, I figured, my uncle and Papa would discuss Rebecca's fate.

I hadn't a prayer of remaining in earshot, since Virginia, somewhat older, had been forced to bed. I made a show of going upstairs to my room, where Daisy pounced.

"What's going to happen?" she asked.

"I don't know yet."

"Time's short," she reminded me. "We've only got until midnight."

"Daisy, I'm doing the best I can." I began to cry.

"Honey, I know. I didn't mean to fuss." She helped me out of the black dress in silence, and left with one sympathetic hug.

Fortunately, the men left the library to bid the ladies farewell;

by the time I'd changed into nightclothes, the three of them had settled in the warmer parlor to smoke and talk.

I'd long since discovered that if the hall door stayed open, conversation from the parlor wafted up the stairwell to the upper hallway. It was not my favored way to eavesdrop, since my sisters might pop out of their room at any time. But, tonight it would have to serve. I crouched behind the balustrade.

To my dismay, the conversation concerned death, which I had heard plenty of already. Then it lingered on boyhood memories, which ordinarily I would have enjoyed. Finally, Papa said, "Carter, how long can you stay?"

"Not long. To the weekend at most. That profitless Peace Conference ate up weeks, and now the political situation is so hot I can't afford to be out of town for long."

There was a pause, doubtless while they sucked their cigars. A curl of blue smoke wafted into the hall.

My uncle began to describe Richmond, where bands were marching night and day to cheers. Tempers were running so high that Northern merchants took to hanging Southern colors over their storefronts, hoping this display of loyalty would ward off vandals. As for those men who'd formerly opposed slavery, Uncle Carter said "they appear to be in real danger."

At last, he addressed the topic I'd waited for.

"Landon, the temper of the times is such that, well, Monty turned me down on trading Rebecca back. Ordinarily he'd have been persuadable, I think. Right now, he feels lucky she's no longer his problem."

"You can't see your way to freeing her yourself?" Papa's voice was sad and strained, but no longer angry. "Felicity's already heard from her sister. Her Meeting's agreed to sponsor the girl. Sapphire and her family are real set on this, too."

Winston Wright, who'd clearly been told about the problem, spoke up. "Lan, you can't expect that. Emma sees a lady's maid as necessary for Virginia's marriage portion." The sound of Mr. Wright pacing the floor reached me, then his voice, much louder. "Obviously you can't trade Daisy. That was a stupid idea, as Carter himself now agrees. But, Lan, you mustn't let your soft spot for your slaves rule your life."

The voice diminished as he moved toward the fireplace. "Be sensible. Both of you. Landon, this girl is nothing to your family. You don't owe her. Being lady's maid to your niece is hardly a harsh fate.

"As for you, Carter, take the girl home. You made the deal, and you should handle the consequences, though they're awkward."

Mr. Wright's voice was loud again. I figured he'd turned his back to the fire to lecture. "Now put this quarrel behind you. No chit of a slave is worth argument between brothers."

"I reckon you're right," Papa said, defeated.

I tiptoed down the hall, skipped the squeaky plank, headed for the back stairs. I could reach Pearl, in her room off the kitchen, and she'd relay my news to the quarters.

I was almost too tired to keep moving.

I absolutely believed Daisy that sending any slave from this plantation tonight was uncommonly risky. I admired Rebecca as a person. I feared for her as a female. I had promised her help. Yet I was no longer the person who'd thoughtlessly, almost lightheartedly, volunteered for adventure after our tea party.

My feet slowed, and I leaned against the wall to think. Should I put everyone I loved in peril?

I envied Isabel and Nelly, those know-nothings asleep with clean consciences. Why, oh *why*, did I keep poking my nose in things I then regretted knowing?

From the Blue Room came the sound of a muffled argument. Without even a thought of resisting temptation, I set my ear to the door's crack.

Someone was tugging on the doorknob, fit to break the thing. "You've locked us in!" Rebecca's voice was panic-stricken. "Why'd you do that? We could be burnt in our beds!"

"You've been sneaking off at night. When I want you, I don't want to chase you."

"Please. I need the outhouse."

"You're lying. You're going to the quarters." Big sigh. "I'll surely be glad to get home for a dozen reasons—one being that you won't go wandering." The sound of Virginia flouncing on the bed seeped through the door. "At home you stick to me like a burr; here, I mostly can't find you. Now, get back in the trundle before you freeze."

"Please, Miss Virginia?"

"Now, you listen to me, gal. The Negroes around here have been giving you uppity ideas. You watch yourself, or I'll sell you right off and buy someone reliable."

The trundle squeaked as Rebecca climbed into it. I turned to leave; time was short, and I'd promised to let Daisy know.

Then Rebecca spoke again. "What would I cost, Miss?"

"You got any money?"

"No. I just wondered."

"Well, I heard Mr. Montcure promise Papa he'd be getting a 'true diamond' when he traded for you. So, I guess you're worth more than most gals your age. You got a diamond to buy yourself with?" Virginia began to chuckle at the idea.

"No, ma'am, I don't." This time, the sigh was Rebecca's.

I started down the hall, toward Pearl's room, with news I dreaded to tell. Yet I couldn't fail Daisy and Sapphire—or, for that matter, Pearl, Ruby, and Horace. They were waiting for me, holding up the train. How could I say Rebecca wouldn't be left with us and also couldn't escape?

Seemed the whole terrible day collapsed on me and squashed me toward the floor. I ached to have Baby Bea back, and, I confess, I wanted my mama as much as a small child would.

I crept to my parents' bedroom and slipped inside the partly open door. The oil lamp was low, but would burn till Papa came to bed. Mama lay unmoving, but her eyes were open.

"You all right, Mama?"

She didn't move, or answer, but her eyes blinked, to my relief. I moved closer, but her expression was blank. She wasn't seeing me at all. How long could this last? I was frightened. She had been dressed, propped up, and supported by other people for three days and had now collapsed entirely.

I must leave. It's near midnight. I have to tell Pearl.

I couldn't. I just couldn't face another evil thing.

I had to *do* something. Something to prove to myself that I had power enough, *right now,* to change this dreadful day into one worth living. Briefly, I considered calling some lie through Virginia's door to get Rebecca out, but the stupidity of that idea dissuaded me.

Then the Inner Light hit again. I knew what was right to do. It would endanger no one. And I owned the means.

I moved to Mama's bureau, opened her jewel casket, and took my locket. I held the trinket so the diamond sparkled in the lamp glow. It was really big; surely worth a slave.

Then I gathered my courage and went back toward the parlor in my nightclothes. I peered down. Mr. Wright entered the hall below, adjusting his hat to leave; Uncle Carter started walking him toward the verandah door. Sounds of Papa damping the fire came from the parlor.

I drew back. Best to wait till Mr. Wright left.

"Thanks, Winston," Uncle Carter said. "I couldn't have persuaded Lan without your help."

Persuaded Papa to what? I thought.

"Well," Mr. Wright replied, "you two are like brothers to me. I couldn't see him get a reputation for cowardice or Yankee sympathies and not try to convince him to join up right off."

I leaned over the banisters and stretched to hear.

"That was a very good point you made," my uncle said. "Every able-bodied student and master will leave for the war anyway. Might as well enlist and prove his Southern loyalty."

Mr. Wright gave a pleased little laugh. "This'll be good for him. Give him a month or two away from all these wimmin and Quaker ways! The war won't last long, better grab the glory while we can."

They went out the door; a rumble of farewells reached me. I ducked back as my uncle reentered and walked toward the parlor.

How could Papa even think of leaving now, with Mama so sad, and increasing? I comforted myself: *Atha and Sophie will still be here to help.*

I dashed down the stairs to catch the men together before they left for bed. They were startled.

"Why are you up at this hour, child?" asked Papa.

"I couldn't sleep. I kept worrying about Rebecca." I turned to my uncle. "She loves Sapphire and Daisy, and they love her. She says this feels like home. She's crying over leaving. Let her stay, please!"

My uncle nodded. "I know she'd like to, but we can't afford to leave her," he said with surprising gentleness. "We take good care of her."

"Virginia said she'd sell her for a diamond," I pressed on. "Is this enough to buy her?" I held out the locket, and the gem twinkled as the heavy gold orb spun on its chain.

The two men stared at me, silent with shock.

Uncle looked at Papa. "Landon, did you know about this?"

"Lord, no!" Papa shook his head at me. "That's your special legacy, Evvy. You'd regret letting it go. Whatever put this into your head?"

I shrugged. They waited.

"I'd buy Beatrice back, if I could, and make Mama and all of us happy. But I can't. Nobody can. But I can make Sapphire and Daisy and Rebecca happy. How can a *thing*—even an inheritance—weigh against a real person? When that person's gone, it's too late to do any good."

Papa turned aside and rubbed his eyes. "I know," he said. "*Things* seem a mockery, don't they? Bea's tiny shoes . . . her silver baby cup . . . here . . . but she's gone." He turned back, and the misery in his face made him old. "Do as you please, Child. If it makes you feel better, it's a sacrifice well made."

I turned to Uncle, impatient now, rather than scared. "Virginia's always liked this locket. Is it enough?"

I bought Rebecca for the locket.

I slipped off to tell Pearl that the train must leave immediately, that Rebecca was locked in, couldn't escape, but wouldn't be going to Richmond anyway.

"You sure did take your time, Honey," said Pearl. "Horace'll have to run flat-out to get to the rock before midnight."

That night I knelt and prayed my strongest. *Please, Lord, let Mama get better. Don't let war start. Keep Papa home. Make Aunt Honor tell Atha and Sophie to stay. Don't let Mr. Wright run into the Train going home. Keep us all safe, Amen.*

I reckon Mr. Wright never noticed anything that night, since the Railroad went through without trouble. That was all the good prayer did, though.

Twenty-two

In Which I
Acquire a School

WE BURIED Beatrice on Wednesday; on Thursday, shots were fired at Fort Sumter, though we didn't know it. War had begun.

Within a week, we heard that Lincoln had offered Robert E. Lee the command of the Federal Army, but Lee had turned him down. Then the rumor was published news, and Papa called the family into the parlor to read us the general's words.

With all my devotion to the Union and the feeling of loyalty and duty of an American citizen, I have not been able to make up my mind to raise my hand against my relatives, my children, my home.

"That's how I feel," Papa said.

He glanced at Mama, sitting by the fireplace. It was her first visit to that room since the disaster. Other than the missing rug, nothing looked amiss. She remained silent. At first I had hoped the laudanum the doctor had left was responsible for her lassitude, but Sapphire had strictly forbidden its use after a few days. "No telling but it might hurt the coming baby," she said. With that, at least, Mama had agreed. About most things she now had no opinion.

Atha spoke up. "Now that the Virginia Commonwealth has joined the Confederacy, Sophie and I should return home."

"No!" I leapt from my chair. "No. No, please. You promised to stay, at least till the new baby comes."

Atha shook her head. "That's impractical. Pupils will likely withdraw from a school run by Yankees. We don't know when Aunt Felicity will be well enough to teach again, and we might be a real danger for the family if we seem to be in charge here."

She looked from me to Papa, and continued. "I suspect Uncle Landon is about to tell us he'll be joining a regiment."

"That's not true, is it, Papa?" Isabel asked.

"I hadn't intended to speak of that yet," Papa said, with a nervous glance at Mama, "but, yes. Carter and Winston have convinced me that, for our safety, it's the wise course."

He leaned to look at Mama directly. "Felicity, no one believes the war can last more than several months. My older students plan to leave—my faculty, also. Even Newland says he'll seek a desk job in the government at Richmond."

Mama's face remained expressionless, and Papa tried again for a response. "Dearest, listen. Sophie and Atha have managed the Academy's accounts and kept the girls' school open. They've been a great help." He flashed my cousins a look of gratitude. "But they may be leaving."

Mama nodded, the first sign she'd given of hearing anything. "Close both schools for the duration, Landon. I can't run them, and we can't keep Honor's daughters here under the circumstances."

"Oh, no! Please!" burst from me.

Beatrice had died, war had started, Papa was leaving, my cousins talked of deserting, Mama continued unwell. Even the ordinary round of chores had been neglected. The house was dingy, my sisters' hair ill brushed, their seams pinned, not mended, the lamps half black with soot. Meals were soups or stews thrown into a pot, perhaps with pancakes or corn bread, but no raised loaves, few greens, no desserts. The outhouse had begun to reek.

My parents hadn't the energy for even the simplest things. My father's neglect of his favorite job—the winding of the grandfather clock each Sunday—was typical of the depressed indifference of our home. He hadn't wound it the Sunday of Bea's death, or ever after. The spring was too hard for me to wind, and Horace was afraid to set it, "as I don't know my numbers," he said. The hall seemed forlorn without its comforting ticktock.

The fact that we still had Atha and Sophie and school had been my only hope these past weeks. My cousins to lean on, and the routine of learning and teaching would, I hoped, repair our lives. Suddenly, right here in the parlor, even those last resources were in danger.

I knelt on the floor at Mama's feet, and took her hand. "Mama, we must keep Olympus open, even if Atha and Sophie do leave. Isabel and Daisy can take on the junior girls, and I can guide the senior group, if you'll help with planning."

Mama made no response. I glanced at Papa, who looked doubtful. What argument would move him? Desperation brought ideas. I stared at him. "We shouldn't twiddle around, with nothing to do, and the men away. We could even move Olympus into Chamberlyn Hall while you're gone. Then the Jenkinses would be nearby to help, same as with the boys. It would be quiet here for Mama. But, she'd need to help plan classwork, too."

Papa, my cousins, and I had discussed the problem of Mama. Sapphire had been frank, as Mama's lassitude continued. "Miss Felicity's holding on till the baby, but Death hovers over every birthing bed," she'd said. "Don't want Him taking my Miss. She needs quiet to rest, but also needs to perk up. Take an interest."

Sophie spoke up, probably remembering Sapphire's advice. "I think Evvy's right, Uncle. Thee should keep the girls' school going, and everybody busy, no matter what."

Atha nodded. "Income and diversion are both worthwhile." She knelt on the other side of Mama, and took her hand. "Aunt Felicity, do you understand?"

Mama nodded slightly. "Thee and Sophie and Landon are leaving soon. Evvy will put Olympus in the Academy building. She'll keep the girls occupied till Landon gets back."

Her voice was flat, even dreamy. It was not her understanding but her caring that was impaired. I was unnerved by the indifference. Our life was slipping away, faster and faster, as Mama slipped away, too.

Mama pulled her hand away and slid it under the Chinese jacket to hold her stomach. Her eyes brightened a moment. "He kicked," she said. The smile was small, but it was a start.

A year ago, I would have been jealous, both of the baby and that "he," but now relief washed through me. Mama connected to something.

I looked at Atha, and saw she'd realized the same thing. I wasn't going to forgive her promise, though. "You said you'd stay until the baby comes." My jaw was tight. I could hardly move my lips. Underneath, words I couldn't say welled up to be choked back. *You can't leave me to handle everything alone. You promised.*

Atha avoided my eyes. "We'll see," she said. She glanced at her sister. "We have . . . concerns. We must consult our Inner Light before we promise more."

Sophie returned my glance for a second, and tears began to shimmer behind her lashes as she, too, looked away. "We . . . I . . ." Her voice broke, and she ran from the room. Atha rushed after her.

"I'll see what's the matter," I said to Papa, and he nodded.

The door to Olympus was latched tight. I called from the porch, but my cousins didn't answer. Sapphire came out on her stoop, and gestured me over.

"They'll be holding a Meeting," she observed. "They told me they need to sit quiet till the Inner Light comes on them." She shook her head. "Not my way. To my thinking, a joyful noise unto the Lord works better, but . . ."—she shrugged—"they've got a problem neither silence nor noise is going to cure. Come in, Honey. We can set on my settle while we wait."

"Sapphire, what am I to do? Papa's leaving for war, and Mama . . . well, you know." I wiggled back onto Aunt Jane's carved settee, worn smooth by a thousand bottoms, and comforting. I relaxed. Sapphire would know what to do.

Sapphire nodded. "She needs time, Honey."

"Sapphire, there's the rest of us still here. Seems like Mama just stopped caring for anybody but Beatrice. Unless a little for the new baby."

Sapphire leaned her arms on her knees and stared at the floor a minute. "I've cogitated on that, Honey. How come? She loves all her girls, and your papa, too. I expect this is why: She didn't know, down inside, bad things could happen to her own self, and now she does."

She turned to look directly at me. "It doesn't help, blaming herself. It's not like Baby died from fever. She was fine, then dead, and it wasn't God's Will. Can't blame Joycelyn or Annalee. They're hardly more than babies."

"We need Mama so much!" I wailed.

"Honey, we do, for a fact," Sapphire replied. "Chores don't organize themselves, and this property needs a mistress."

"And now, Atha and Sophie say they're leaving, too! Just because this war has started. They promised. They *promised* to stay till the baby comes. How can they leave me—us—now?"

"Honey, I think we've got another baby coming," Sapphire said as she sat up straight. Now she avoided my eyes. "Miss Sophie, I think she's about as far along as your mama."

I stared at her, openmouthed in shock. "She can't be. She's not married. And look how Mama looks—Sophie's not that shape."

"Well, I've been noticing for some time she's been walking like a lady with a baby. Recently, I've been sure." Sapphire glanced at me at last. "She doesn't look like your mama, that's a fact. But this makes seven times for Miss Felicity, and all those things inside that hold up babies stretched easy this time around. Miss Sophie, she's young and tight. You never wondered why she's been wearing those big aprons since Christmas?"

Numbly, I shook my head. "Atha wears them, too," I said. Another thought struck me. "Does Atha know?"

"Now she knows, yes. Only a couple of weeks, though. I saw her getting strained, what with Beatrice, then your mama, then handling the Academy accounts and the school, then the war, and your papa looking to leave. And now this baby. She's pretty well pulled apart inside, I think."

"How could this have happened," I moaned, hardly expecting an answer. I was jolted by a laugh from Sapphire.

"Easy to happen, Honey. Happens all the time."

"It's not funny!" I began to cry. "The baby will be a bastard. That's terrible. Atha told me so."

"Now you listen up, Miss Evelyn Chamberlyn. You've no call to stick a mean name on a child that's not even born yet. No God that put love in the world would sort babies into good and bad piles because a preacher did or didn't marry the parents."

"But the Bible says sins of the fathers are visited upon the children. . . ." A great bubble of misery welled from my stomach up my chest and came out in an odd noise. "Atha told me."

Sapphire slid over on the settee and hugged me. "Honey, Miss Atha's smart and nice, too. But like most White folks, she doesn't think straight on this. You listen to me. If having a preacher-man marry people is so important, why are there laws against Negro folks using one?"

"I don't know." I thought a minute. "I don't think Quakers have a preacher at all. Not even for sermons. So how do they get married?"

"Probably the way Negro folks do. Miss Jane gave my mammy and pappy a preacher wedding, but Julius and me married the usual way. We stood up in front of our relatives and friends and joined hands and pledged how we'd love each other and stick by each other. Mammy had made a special cake, and Pappy'd talked Marse Justin into some wine. Julius, he played some really fine music on his fiddle, and folks danced."

"Then you were married?"

"Maybe not in law. But we were as married as could be. I can feel him still. He'll come home. I'll be here."

Abruptly, her mood changed. "I pin this on your aunt Honor and uncle Paul, not Miss Sophie. Some gals are plumb silly at seventeen, but your mama wasn't, and Sophie's not either. She knows who she wants."

She laughed again. "Honey, these babies aren't cursed, I promise you. That one your mama's carrying is maybe saving her life. You know?"

I nodded.

Sapphire looked at me sideways and added, "You think it's a good thing I got born?"

"Oh, Sapphire," I said, "I don't know what we'd do without you. Yes!"

"Well, I got born without a wedding. I'm not a curse, as far as I can see. Pappy Samson, he loved me like my sisters, and my mammy called us all her jewels. That's how we got our names. We don't know what this baby'll do, yet. But there's some reason it got started. Wait and see."

Twenty-three

In Which We
Prepare for War
and Atha Tells a Secret

IN EARLY June, Uncle Carter wrote that his recruits were joining the troops gathering at Manassas Junction, so Papa and Mr. Wright decided to meet him there in about a month with their student brigade.

The older Academy students had gone home to get outfitted, taking their younger brothers and cousins with them. Classes for the boys had ceased. Those who planned to serve would meet Papa at Manassas to enlist. Meanwhile, the local men and boys, even Papa's faculty, drilled in the side field an hour or so each day, which looked silly at first, but they did improve. Every day more farmers and villagers joined.

The girls' school kept morning hours. Then older girls joined the faculty wives, who had turned the library of the Academy into a sewing room. No one knew quite what Confederate soldiers should wear, but Aunt Emma had sent a sketch from Richmond to show what ladies there were creating. We didn't know to make them gray—the first outfits were blue.

Pearl had always been Mama's sewing assistant. Retiring though she usually was, she directed the labor and designed and cut the patterns. Rebecca became Pearl's "right-hand woman."

Only once had Rebecca tried to thank me. "I'll do good work for you, Miss Evvy," she'd said, breaking into tears and kissing my hand. Both of us had been too embarrassed to face that again.

My relationship with Daisy and her family changed. Sapphire began checking plans with me. "Until your mama improves," she said. "You're head lady now."

Daisy began regularly chatting with me about her brothers and her own dream of someday being a schoolteacher for other Negro girls. "You've gone and gotten more sense than a grasshopper," she teased me. "Used to wonder if you knew to come in out of the rain."

The approval of Sapphire and Daisy and their family was sweet to me, and was, I think, what gave me hope I'd measure up to the job at hand.

And that "job at hand," for me, loomed large. Adulthood frightened me. It was turning out to be a lot more than wearing corsets and refraining from harum-scarum behavior.

Mama's collapse of spirit, Papa's decision to soldier, and my cousins' determination to return North, all made me face the truth: No one else was going to take on the responsibility for the plantation. *Like the clock,* I thought. *The parts work fine, if someone winds it up regularly. Lacking that, it stops.*

I first tried to dump at least the household organization on Sapphire, who looked astonished. "You think I'm going to order my sisters and Horace around? No, ma'am. Nohow do I do that." Her eyes twinkled with amusement. "Not many good things about being a slave, but *not* being a boss is one of them."

"I'm stuck, then," I said.

"Yes, ma'am, you are," she said. "You'll do fine."

I now discovered how easy life had been for us girls. Not, of course, as compared with Liza, but the adults had spared us by handling most work themselves.

Atha and Sophie, who'd been running the girls' school and keeping the Academy accounts, began instructing me in these skills. That was hard, but household management was worse.

The "plantation" was actually now a small farm, which supported the family, servants, and boarding students. We were seriously understaffed by the standards of our neighbors.

The Wrights, for instance, had a White overseer and a Negro driver to see to acres of crops and dozens of animals, tended by slaves. Perhaps several hundred slaves. Of house servants, as many as twenty served a family of four persons.

On our property, meals for family, servants, and boarding students caused unremitting work. An endless parade of buckets carried water from the pump for cooking and washing. Logs had to be trimmed to fit the stove, in all seasons.

Vegetables were gathered, chopped, peeled, and cooked. Biscuits or corn bread baked daily. Yeast loaves and several dozen pies were turned out weekly. Root vegetables, fruits, and gourds, if unbruised, were straw-wrapped for storage in the root cellar until winter.

Outhouses needed regular liming, and a constant supply of kernelless corncobs for cleanliness. Oil lamps needed cleaning and trimming after each use. Candlemaking was a four-times-yearly chore. Soap was made from lard renderings at intervals, as we ran out. Butter churning, paddling, and salting took several hours every few days.

On Saturdays, Horace (and often our father) wrestled the rain barrel that caught the soft rainwater off the roof into the kitchen, for bathing and hair washing.

Laundry, on Mondays, started when Horace and his sons lit

a fire under a "witches' cauldron," where clothes and linens were boiled and bleached, as the boys circulated the mass with sticks. The women wrung out and hung pounds of wet fabric on lines between trees. If the sun smiled, these could be gathered and sprinkled for the next day's ironing. In winter, material froze stiff until the wind flapped it dry. At least fifty garments—dresses, petticoats, pantaloons—would need pressing on Tuesdays, and sheets and pillowcases for all.

Tuesdays were equally hard. Several boards were set up outside in summer, which was cooler for the women ironing. But then Josh and Toby had a longer run with hot flatirons from the stove. When an iron cooled, it went back to reheat; the boys ran the circle all day. Isabel and I had sorted, folded, and returned items to drawers or clothespresses for years, but Nelly and Joycelyn would now have to do that.

Many items needed mending. Hand-me-downs became fragile with use. On Wednesdays, Pearl darned stockings and lace, resewed seams, and patched or turned sheets getting thin in the middle. The rest of us dusted, mopped, turned featherbeds, flapped rugs.

Lately, these chores had been skimped. We slept on the same linen for weeks, on unironed sheets. My sisters wore the same dresses repeatedly; Annalee and Joycelyn seemed to mop up dirt.

Every day the men had milking, feeding of livestock, wood-cutting, and shepherding—inescapable chores even on holidays. Cutting and hauling wood was a never-ending chore, and the garden required work from plowing in early spring, then planting, weeding, and harvesting as the year progressed. Heaven preserve us from a dry summer and the task of watering! Papa rented, borrowed, or traded labor, plows, and mules from neighbors to help with some of this work.

Someone had to delegate, borrow, repay, order supplies, keep books, and deal with the problems of farming and schooling and getting meals on the tables. Mama had ceased to care; Papa increasingly escaped to the drilling field; Atha and Sophie were passing duties along, not taking on more. None of the staff, not even Sapphire or the Jenkins ladies, could read or write, or deal with neighbors.

So, even men's work would need to be organized by me, once Papa left. Where was lime kept? Whose job was the outhouse?

My sisters were not much help, but they did do war work. Isabel sewed tirelessly, and even Nelly and Joycelyn joined the women's efforts.

Joycelyn purely hated to sew. She knit socks till the heel needed turning, then asked Mama to do that section before she added the cuff. Since every pair needed Mama's attention, every turned heel was to the good.

Joycelyn presented her first pair to Win, who bowed from the waist and said, "Thank you, Miss Sock-Angel. An army travels on its feet, you know." She was thrilled and promised to keep him in socks throughout the war.

"Are you flirting with my baby sister, these days?" I teased him, as we met in the sewing room several days later. "You're becoming quite a cradle robber. She's enchanted."

"Why, Miss Evvy, I hadn't any such intent," he drawled. "But, seeing it makes you jealous, I reckon I'll have to give it a try." He looked thoughtfully skyward. "And that Joycelyn's a taking little girl. Reminds me of someone—I wonder who?"

"Why, Mr. Wright, you do flatter yourself," I said. "But, practice makes perfect, and I suppose every young lady you add to your list gets you to your goal of charming us all."

He moved closer and murmured, "Hmm. Intriguing thought. Too bad this room is full of people, not necessarily minding their own business." He cut his eyes toward Nelly, who was alert to catch each syllable.

Such moments of lighthearted relief were few, however. Atha and Sophie taught me accounting. I followed Papa and Horace around, to absorb male skills as well. Each morning, in imitation of Mama's former pattern, I met with the staffs of the Big House and the Academy to assign tasks for the day.

I said nothing about Sophie's baby, but I think Atha suspicioned I knew, because I stopped pressing them to stay. Atha was wild to be off, and daily discussed plans for leaving.

Trains no longer ran from Richmond to Washington and Philadelphia. Southern lines were full of troops, often rowdy, even drunken. A trip by two young women alone, daring the year before, now would be scandalous, even dangerous.

Atha and I discussed Justin's grand coach, which was well sprung and elegantly appointed inside. "It's still in good shape," I said, "though old. And so large it can carry us all to Church in our best clothing. You'd be comfortable, even on so long a journey as Philadelphia. But we can't spare Horace to drive it. He'll soon be the only man on the place."

Atha agreed. "And could he get home again, once he had no White passengers to vouch for him? Rumors of free men being pressed back into slavery are common. We can't risk him."

Though I knew Atha was unhappy, I didn't guess how deeply. I stumbled upon the truth by purest accident.

I'd left Papa and Horace in the office, hoping to find Sophie and review infant class needs. As I reached the porch of Olympus, Mr. Rawley burst out the door without seeing me, slamming his hat on his head as he ran. He was visibly shaken, muttering something on the order of *GodhelpmeohGodhowcan Istandit?*

I grabbed the door in midswing, and saw Atha shaking with sobs and clinging to the dictionary stand as if her very bones had melted. At her feet lay four thick volumes, forming a barrier.

"Atha!" I ran, pried her fingers from the stand and led her around the books to the teaching bench. "What's wrong? I could kill Mr. Rawley. What did he say?" For a mad moment, I imagined he'd discovered Sophie's secret and condemned her to Atha.

"No, oh, no! He didn't hurt me." She shook her head. "I mean . . . maybe he did, but he didn't mean to." She wiped her face on the student hand towel, hiding a rising blush, and then gave a tremulous smile.

"In fact," she said, "in the oddest way, I am happier than I've ever been." She sniffed. Caught her breath. Dabbed her eyes. "Can you keep a secret?" she asked.

I nodded. I was as good at secret keeping as anyone could well be; of this I was sure.

"It's perhaps wrong of me, but I need to tell someone." Her eyes pleaded with me. I was thrilled to nod agreement.

"Mr. Rawley loves me." Atha's face shone with pride and excitement. "He would never have told me, but he's off to war, and I to Philadelphia, and we shall never meet again. He brought me"—here she broke down and wept a bit—"volume four. And he brought back volumes one through three. I'm to keep the whole set to remember him by."

So that explained *The Rise and Fall of the Roman Empire.*

"But he's married!" I blurted, forgetting that I myself had doubted he had genuine affection for his wife.

"Yes." Atha sat straight. "Perhaps that's the greatest blessing of all, hard though it seems. I can never have any right to him, and I've never dreamed I could. So I have the love of a man such as I never imagined I could—I didn't know I could feel so . . . so . . . It is beyond anything!"

Her eyes shone, as she turned to me. "I have gained much, but lost nothing."

Quietly, she added, "I've never planned to marry, and I know the life of a wife is not the one for me." She smiled a bit, though sadly, and added, "My mama and yours have managed to have some satisfaction beyond children and family, but most women cannot." Here she gave me a quick smile. "And, then, our papas are unusually broadminded."

I thought of Aunt Honor's letter: "There is Sacrifice in Marriage for women, or we should not feel so about it." Out loud I said, "For Sophie, marriage will be a joy. For you—"

"For me, a sacrifice of everything I plan to do with my life. Clayton is the finest man I could wish for." Here she blushed red again. "But even he would not understand. He would expect"—she glanced at me—"as your papa does—as mine does—that he and any children we had must come first."

I nodded. Men could put work or country before family. Papa was, right now. But that would not be tolerated in a wife.

I knew this as surely as Atha did.

Twenty-four

In Which I
Bid Farewell to Romance

ON THE last day of May, as preparations for the men's departure drew to a close, I saw Liza ride up to the drilling field, dismount, and watch the horsemen through the fence. She looked oddly forlorn, and I decided to slip away to join her.

"I'm not bragging when I say I *am* the best rider in the county, male or female, even riding sidesaddle," she grumbled, as the men charged by us. "It's vastly unfair that Papa and Win are peacocking in uniform, headed for glory, while I'm stuck here doing nothing."

She sighed. "I'm not even a tolerable seamstress; I drop stitches when I knit, and Mama refuses to consider sending me to Richmond to comfort wounded soldiers, should there be any." Restlessly, she paced the fence, staring at the drill. "Your aunt Emma would take me in, I know she would."

I shook my head. "There you're wrong. Aunt Emma wrote asking us to keep Virginia and Georgia for the duration of the war. She said, 'Gently raised young ladies should not be exposed to the Streets of what is now the Confederate Capital.' "

With some excitement, I added, "Papa says four Academy families have written to ask us to admit their daughters. If the war goes on, he predicts there'll be more. Who knows? Maybe Olympus will fill the Academy building up, instead of rattling around in the extra space."

"Lordy, lordy, Evvy. However will you abide living with a bunch of spoiled creatures who'll hate being stuck in the country as much as I do? And with your cousins leaving? *Pahh.*" She snorted her contempt for the plan.

"Well, I told Papa I'd not endure Virginia, or even Georgia, no matter how short this war may be. But we do need income, Liza, and Papa's said I may use the Academy after the men leave."

Liza looked at me in astonishment. "You sound as if you *like* the idea." She pressed a hand to my forehead. "Are you sick? Or merely insane?"

"I don't yet know how I'll manage. But the Jenkinses can cook and clean for girls as well as boys. Their boys will go, too, so they've agreed to move into Chamberlyn Hall to monitor. And we'll have the Academy library! We'll be able to offer a full course of studies."

Liza gave me that arch look. "My dear Evelyn, you must watch yourself. You're looking two years older this last month— it ain't improving you!"

I was in no mood to be teased. "Liza, you complain of boredom—I get no rest, and not likely to soon. Come help if you will, but stop poking me to idle with you." My eyes teared with self-pity. "I guess I will be a dried-up old prune and unmarriageable in a month or two, at that."

"I'm sorry, Evvy." She gave me a hug. "I was mean to tease. I know you have a full plate at present." She gave another sideways glance. "You don't need to worry about beaux—I know for a fact. Speaking of which," she continued, "I see a certain beau approaching. One who will *not* be thrilled to have his sister lurking nearby." She stepped on the fence rail, bounced upward, thrust her foot in the stirrup and settled into the sidesaddle. "Now, be sweet to him," she admonished. "He's off to war, after all!" She blew a kiss and cantered off.

Win was walking his horse to cool it after the drill and motioned me to join him. I moved to the stile, mounted the steps, and sat on the top to chat.

Most men were like Liza, positively thrilled over the coming war. Even Papa eagerly anticipated it now, though in his case I suspect it meant getting away from our sad house. Win, however, realized war was serious; he also empathized with my fear that I couldn't cope with both school and plantation.

"How are things, Evvy?" he asked.

"Oh . . . fine," I said. "All our folks are willing and hard working. If I keep my head on straight, we should manage."

Win was army-bound and I ought not to burden him further with my fears. I should tease him from his mood. I smiled. "Once Olympus moves into the Academy, we women will spread out and take over. *While the cat's away, the mice will play.*"

He did not smile back.

"What's the matter?" I asked. He rubbed his eyes and looked away.

"There must be something wrong with me," he said to the distance. "The other men say they can hardly wait to kill a Billy Yank."

He turned to me, his brow twisted. "I'd never turn tail and run," he said. "At least, I feel pretty sure I won't. But I can't imagine shooting or bayoneting another man. Looking him in the face and doing that. Finding the picture of his wife and child in his pocket."

"Maybe it's the Quaker blood in me," I answered, "but I believe it takes more courage to refuse to kill than to kill."

He looked a little hurt. "I could never refuse to serve," he said. "Quakers may be pacifist, but I can't do that."

"I know," I said, "I know." I patted his hand. "But there's nothing wrong or unmanly in not wanting to kill another human being."

THE next evening was the final one before the departure of our warriors to Manassas Junction. The Wrights had scheduled a splendid send-off—a banquet, with dancing and fireworks. This last item was available because their traditional lavish Fourth of July celebration had been cancelled for this year.

It was quite the most elegant dinner party I'd yet attended; the women in their finest, the men in uniforms worn for the first time.

Win invited me to walk to the rose garden and cool off after dancing.

I admit, I thought it would be very fine if Win should kiss me in the dark; I'd come to regret that missed kiss at the Christmas Ball, as I thought of months ahead with no male company and no chance of flirtation.

This evening we'd all striven to be gay. Papa had allowed me a glass of sherry, saying, "If you are going to work as an adult, you should also enjoy some adult privileges."

Then I sneaked a second glass. I was light-headed, and even, for the moment, lighthearted. I figured I deserved a bit of tomfoolery before I was old and pruney.

I felt breathless, from excitement more than from the dancing or the sherry, as we went down the steps from the back verandah to the lawn. The moon glazed the gravel path before us into silver; the early June roses were at the height of their perfumery; and the music from the Wrights' ballroom, softened by distance, seemed to waft from fairyland musicians.

As we reached the pavilion at the garden's end, a rocket soared over the rooftop and showered the night with an umbrella of gold and silver sparks. I could not have devised a more perfect moment for a first kiss, if I'd planned for it. I almost believed I had.

And the kiss was a great success. Neither wet and smoochey nor brisk and peckish as Liza had warned me kisses might be. Win's kiss was firm but gentle, and long enough so that the first little shock had time to turn into a tingle on my lips. Bubbly feelings rose in me.

When we parted, I was the one who leaned forward for a second kiss, and I believe I snuggled in for a squeeze, as well. I surely didn't feel obliged to make a man about to face dangers of war feel unappreciated.

So Win did have encouragement.

But neither Liza's hints nor Win's flirtations and confidences had prepared me to find him on bended knee before me, holding out his grandmother's ruby ring, and saying, "Evvy, wait for me. Please give me a reason to come home."

On the one hand, my body was tingling and urging me to say, "Yes! Oh, yes!" In which case I could count absolutely on more delightful things taking place. On the other hand, my excitement cooled at the thought of being in Sophie's dilemma—or even just at having my future settled forever.

I stepped back.

Win rose, pulled me to him, and kissed me again. "Darling," he murmured into my ear, and began kissing my neck. I felt limp. I had a flashing vision of Atha, collapsed over the dictionary stand, and I knew she'd been thoroughly kissed just before I found her.

I pulled away. "Win. Win. Listen." I was flattered, hated to hurt him, and my mind grappled for a good excuse. "Win. This isn't right. We're too young for this. Papa would never—"

He pulled at my waist again, clamping me close to him. "It *is* right, Evvy. Mama even gave me the ring for you. It's only an engagement; we'll get older soon."

He smiled, inches away from my face. "We both know our fathers have been thinking we'd be a good match since the day you were born. Liza can hardly wait to be your bridesmaid."

I remembered Liza's hint the day before.

"You've already told people?" This was worse than I'd feared.

How horrible it would be for Win to admit I'd turned him down. Miserable for me, when my sisters and Liza teased me for a fool. Sad to face Papa's disappointment. For Win was right: After three generations of close friendship, a marriage would please the families. Win would be so wealthy, he had no need of a dowry. His parents would approve. Indeed, they already *had.*

He smiled a possessive smile. "Pretty much told everybody, but not your family. I didn't want to risk Nelly telling you before I could propose as a surprise, at the right time." He looked from me to the moonlit scene around us with satisfaction. "Could you ever imagine a more perfect moment than this?"

That bit of self-congratulation on his part revived me. I quite understood it—I'd felt it myself.

"Win! Listen to me." I pulled away again. "Here, give me your hand."

He stopped pulling at my waist, and put his hand in mine. This time we were both ungloved, and the warmth of his clasp felt safe. One last wave of regret went through me. Having Win to depend on would make life easy, and my family happy.

Yet I couldn't say yes. I had to find a kind way to say no, for I did care for him and he'd paid me a great honor.

I was stone-cold sober now. Not a trace of sherry left. "Win, I don't mean to marry."

I'd actually never thought that before, but the words seemed nicer than "I don't want to marry you."

"Nonsense," he said. "All girls mean to marry. What else would you do? Live in Isabel's house someday?" Suddenly his face clouded. "Is there somebody you like better than me?"

I shook my head. He released my hand and went back to pulling me to him. I jerked away this time. "Stop."

"Don't get missish on me," he said. "You know you liked it. I'm leaving tomorrow, and we're wasting precious time."

I jerked away again as he pulled at me. "Winston Wright, you listen to me," I said between set teeth. I stamped my foot. "You never asked *me* how I felt. I don't care how many other people you asked, it's up to me. And I say no."

He began to laugh. "Is that it? You're right. I should have guessed that'd make you bristle. Pardon, Darling. I apologize." He went down on his knee again. "Miss Chamberlyn, I will never tell anybody else first again, and may I have the honor of your hand in marriage, please, ma'am?"

He looked sweet in the moonlight. And he was sweet. And he was leaving for the war, maybe never to return. And I had enjoyed every kiss and squeeze.

I shook my head. "Win," I said, "I would never give satisfaction. I'm not cut out to be a wife. Not yours. Not anybody's."

The words were out now, and I knew they were true. I was

like Great-aunt Jane. The very thought of pledging obedience repulsed me.

I felt so sad.

"But you liked it. I know you did." He was hurt and puzzled. He pulled the ring from his pocket again, and held it out hopefully.

I sat down beside him on the grass—hoops be damned. I took the ring from his hand, slipped it into his pocket again, and patted his knee.

"Win, I did like what we did. I maybe even love you, but maybe it's just flirting and kissing I love. I hear other girls talk about love, and I can't figure how they know they are *in it*, and not just wanting to marry. Which I don't."

I grabbed Win's hand again, and squeezed it, hard, for comfort. "I don't plan to raise Isabel's children. I don't like anybody better than you. I just can't live the life wives have to live."

From somewhere inside me rose words I'd never known were there. "I don't want to bear infants. I don't want to raise children. I don't want to have to ask for permission all the time. I don't want a husband deciding my life."

"But I said I was sorry."

"I know. But you couldn't help it. You'd do it again; it's natural that you would."

I blinked back tears, and said what I now knew was true: "Win, you'll make a fine husband for the right girl. I'm different. I'm never going to make a good wife. Not for anybody. Never."

Twenty-five

In Which School, War, Marriage, and Childbirth Collide

THE REST of June turned hot and sticky. We heard that on the tenth there'd been fighting at Big Bethel Church, just above Hampton. Rumors of other encounters and booming sounds in the distance made us wonder—thunder? or cannon?

More girls arrived each week. Papa had been right. As boys streamed from schools into uniform, girls were hustled into academies to keep them from danger. The dormitory over-flowed, and I moved younger boarders into the Jenkinses' house.

Sophie continued serenely teaching the infant class, as her sister fumed over leaving. Mrs. Newland, formerly so vapid, vol-unteered and became animated among babies. That solved the problem of a replacement when Sophie left.

What truly boggled *my* mind was the transformation of Mrs. Rawley. Faced with a manless world and boredom, she recalled her excellent French. She came to teaching with a secret supply of French novels. I couldn't help smiling at the thought of them nestled up against *The Decline and Fall of the Roman Empire* on some bookcase.

I remembered that the Reverend-lecturer had particularly forbidden novels as weakening to female minds. I therefore decided to test the theory by letting the students escape the tedium and terror of the war with novel-reading. Not surprisingly, French became a favorite class and the girls improved rapidly, as only advanced students could borrow the books.

Liza had been partly right. Though most girls enjoyed the sociability of school, some, of courting age, were keenly aware of losing precious time. And bored. And angry.

When I taught the oldest group Cavalier poetry, I had a near-riot on my hands. Robert Herrick in "To the Virgins, to Make Much of Time" advises to "gather ye rose-buds while ye may, Old Time is still a flying" and ends with:

> *Then be not coy, but use your time;*
> *And while ye may, go marry:*
> *For having lost but once your prime,*
> *You may forever tarry.*

A few weeks later I discovered this ditty scratched into the oak paneling of the dormitory, and read it aloud in class:

> *O my life! What a strife!*
> *I wish I was a soldier's wife.*

When I pointed out that it should read "I wish I *were* a soldier's wife," the group exploded in laughter, then in tears. The rest of the hour they argued over who suffered most—married women, fearing for a particular man, or girls like themselves, threatened with no husband at all.

Atha spent most of her time managing, billing, buying, directing staff—and teaching me to follow her. She still met with the older girls. I worried, as several were my age. Even older. They were well behind me in studies, but would they listen to me?

Daisy and Rebecca taught the younger grades; I needed competent staff. Rebecca's appearance was more Italian or Spanish than Negro; she could pass as White. I thanked Heaven I'd stood firm against admitting Virginia and Georgia, who would surely have raised a fuss. No one objected, praise God. Most youngsters had recently been ruled by mammies and were comfortable with the arrangement.

I had tried to persuade Rebecca to go North with my cousins, whenever we figured out how to get them home. She'd flatly refused.

"It's not just gratitude to you, Miss Evelyn," she said, when pushed. "This is home, here. I don't want to start over somewhere new. Not now. I can teach and cook and clean and sew and do all kinds of things to be useful." She paused, and looked at me more boldly than usual. "You won't force me, will you?"

I had a moment of recognition. I was near to insisting she agree. Just what I hated when Papa, not to mention other men, tried to do it to me. Rebecca had the right to her own decisions, though I thought I knew better.

"Sorry, Rebecca. Of course you can stay."

I'd learned a good deal about Rebecca, mostly relayed by Daisy. With me and my family she was still shy, but I often heard her chatting and laughing in the kitchen.

Old Mrs. Montcure had spent the better part of her declining years educating the girl. By day, Rebecca had been a lady's companion. By night, she slept in the quarters with a woman she fondly called Grannymammy.

The trunk of clothing remained a mystery. Rebecca shrugged and said, "It was like Miss Adelaide to do a kindness and keep it for a surprise."

One day, as I helped Daisy and Rebecca get ready for class, I asked her, "What happened to Grannymammy?"

"Miss Adelaide freed all her folks in her Will, and left some money, too. They went out to the country and bought a farm together. Last I heard, they were fine."

"Why didn't she free you, then?"

"Seems I belonged to her son. He'd just loaned me. Left me there at age two. I spent fourteen years with Miss Adelaide. So, when she died, I went to his house till he traded me away."

Daisy emitted a sound of disgust. "She owed you more than that! She was probably your grandma. You've surely figured that out, girl!"

Rebecca drew herself up. "Daisy, I won't hear one thing against her. She always said she'd 'see to me,' but she died so suddenly. . . ." Her face began to crumple; she put down the papers she was sorting and went to stare from the window.

"That last morning . . . we were having tea . . . she dropped her cup and keeled over the table. I pulled her upright, screamed for help, and she . . . she looked right at me and said, 'Forgive me, Dear Child, I delayed too long. . . .' Then her head dropped, and Grannymammy rushed in, but . . . she was gone."

We fell silent, letting her recover. Daisy finally muttered, "Well, I still say she should've done *something*."

She turned to stare at me, crossing her arms over her chest. "White women don't like these goings-on any better than Negro folks do. Why don't they help us? Keep their men in line? Tell them to behave and make them do it."

I stared back. Keep men in line?

I'd been working to escape being kept in line myself, avoiding the life laid out for me. But to tell Papa directly—or even that idiot Reverend—what *he* had to do or how *he* had to live had not crossed my mind. Ladies didn't.

With the possible exception of Great-aunt Jane.

A new world opened before my eyes. What if I had said, "Papa, I forbid you to leave." Or, "Uncle, it is your Christian duty to free Rebecca." Could I have publicly condemned Spottswood, reputation be damned?

Daisy and I faced each other as seconds passed. I shook my head. "I don't know. I really don't know why."

———

JULY wore on. We stopped classroom work; it was too hot. The students sat under the trees and sewed or knitted for the war effort, listening to improving books.

Since there were no men around, except Horace, I decided to let the girls go to Fat Creek in shifts, and use the swimming hole to cool off. They could also wash their own laundry and dry it on the Big Rock while they played.

Within a fortnight, some were skinny-dipping, swinging from the rope into the pond. Nearly all wore cool braids and cotton dresses, omitting underpinnings.

Papa wrote from Manassas that Confederate troops had swelled to 30,000 men, and a similar number of Yankees had gathered. "It won't be long now," he wrote. "We're impatient."

Mama occasionally visited the sewing room and regularly turned heels for Joycelyn, but never asked about school or war and looked about to burst. Even Sophie now looked fat and awkward in the oversized aprons. *How can it be that no one else notices?* I wondered. Atha got more nervous daily. Fear for Sophie and her baby-to-be, pity for Mama, and yearning after Mr. Rawley combined to lay low even her stalwart spirit. Atha was constituted to *do* something about problems, but these particular miseries couldn't be solved by action.

———

"Sapphire," I said, "what's going on? Mama hardly moves and Sophie's energetic, but they both seem so . . . so *disconnected.* Atha's frantic; I'm worried. It's not *fair* for them to be serene!"

Sapphire looked up from the bread she was kneading and chuckled. "Fair! Lordy, child. You'll have to scold old Ma Nature about that. They're in those last days. Putting everything into bringing those babies to full-time delivery. Worries would waste their energy."

"Sapphire." She stopped kneading and raised an eyebrow at me. "*When* are these babies coming? We've got to prepare. Sophie can't get to Philadelphia in time now, can she? Atha will have to wait till the birth is over. And the students mustn't know. An unwed mother for a teacher would ruin the school. What are we to do?"

Sapphire shrugged. "My part's done: herbs ready, and the kitchen set up. Got the little birthing room clean, and the soft stuff for bundling." She patted my shoulder. "Honey, I plan to get those babies here safely. After that, what happens is up to you. Or up to God. One way or another, things work out."

I had hoped Sapphire would tell me what to do, but I wasn't surprised when she wouldn't. Part of me was scared silly, but part was proud she relied on me, same as on God, to get us through our crises.

———

The first news from Manassas seemed rosy. It had been a defeat for the North. Liza rode over from Wright's Rest, carrying letters sent by special messenger. She burst into the office late in the afternoon, to recount the news her father had written her mother.

"Seems like at the beginning neither side could get advantage. But, then . . . !"

Liza paused for effect, and her eyes shone as she recounted the glories. "A South Carolinian named General Bee spotted General Jackson and his men in line of battle on the edge of a thicket. He pointed toward them, and yelled, 'Look! There stands Jackson like a stone wall! Rally behind the Virginians!' Oh, Evvy, our State turned the tide of battle!"

Liza twirled with excitement. "And guess what?"

"What?"

"Those blue uniforms we sewed helped—the Yankees thought the Virginians were Union soldiers, because they weren't wearing gray." She giggled with delight, quite forgetting that she'd never taken a single stitch herself.

"When they found out, the Yankees broke and ran, and old General McDowell beat a retreat over the Bull Run, with our boys hollering after him.

"Then . . ."—she paused again for effect—"a cart overturned and blocked the bridge, and of all things, hundreds of *picnickers,* who'd come out from Washington to watch, panicked—the Yankee troops stumbled over them to escape. It must've been a hoot! Oh, I wish I'd been there! Why was I born a girl?"

Of course, there was a bad side to this glorious victory. The brunt of the fighting had fallen to the Virginian generals Johnston and Jackson, and our group of soldiers had been in the midst of the fray.

There were casualties.

Liza handed me a letter from Papa. I glanced quickly over its crowded lines, as she jiggled impatiently, then read aloud.

My dear Evelyn. I thought I should write myself to reassure you, and let you select a good moment to tell Mama and the other girls. I have sustained a leg wound, nothing serious. Your Uncle and Dabney and Winstons, both Sr. and Jr., are fine. Montcure, Carter's college friend, is the only other of the grown men of our troop hit, though he declares it is the merest scratch. Several of our former students are injured, and young Gibson is not like to live. I am in hopes your cousins have found safe escort to Philadelphia; if not, please give my fondest regards. I am of course anxious to hear that your Dear Mama is well, and delivered of a healthy infant. If you have a chance to send news, tell the messenger that I will pay well for delivery. Of course, my best love to all my girls. I close in haste to catch Winston's messenger.
Yr. ever-devoted Papa

A second letter, addressed to me in Uncle Carter's sprawling hand, had worse news.

My dear Niece. I hate to place yet another burden on your young shoulders, but your father (in a very natural desire to save you worry) has understated his danger. His wound shows signs of infection, and I am sending him (& some boys, too) to Richmond while he can still ride, in care of Dabney. Montcure will lead, as he lives but a few squares from me, & can stop with his wife to get patched. We do not trust these army doctors, nor, indeed,

doctors at all. If possible, send Sapphire immediately, as
Emma is not talented with injury. Hoping this finds you
well, and your Mama safely through her travail,
Yr. loving Uncle Carter

"What will you do?" Liza asked. "Your uncle wouldn't ask for Sapphire lightly. He knows you can't spare her. Or Horace, to take her."

I slumped over the desk and shook my head. "I don't know. Aunt Emma's worse than hopeless, but I can't send Sapphire yet. Not until after the babies come."

"Babies? Does Sapphire predict twins for your mama?"

I mumbled something, then said, "Liza, would you do me the favor of telling the students about the Manassas victory? You do it so well. It's almost suppertime, so you can announce it in the refectory. I must go to the Big House with Papa's news."

She was off, question forgotten, eager to spread the word. The students went into a frenzy of hero-worship, and Stonewall Jackson was immortalized from that day forward.

Twenty-six

In Which
Providence Intervenes
and Sophie Is Married

SAPPHIRE agreed. "I can't go till the babies come, but that should be mighty soon. Ruby or Daisy can do aftercare, but not these deliveries. Your mama's delicate. Miss Sophie's healthy as a horse, but it's her first. You never know about the first."

She shook her head. "No siree. Got to be here." She gave a brisk nod. "Think I'll give those babies a shove. We're so close now, it should work. I'll cogitate." The screen door slammed as she went down the back stoop to her herb storage.

I joined my family for supper, told about Manassas, then described Papa's injury as he had—a minor wound. I didn't share Uncle Carter's fear of infection or his plea for Sapphire. The men had trusted me, and I wouldn't burden Mama or Sophie with fear of losing the midwife or guilt at keeping her.

Mama took the news almost too easily. "If a wound will allow him to come home with honor, that would be fine."

Pearl served tea with chips of ice to everyone but Mama and Sophie; Sapphire set special glasses at their places, then gave me a grave nod. Her lips formed the word "tonight."

In the heat of the July evening, I escaped to the verandah to rock, stare at the dusk, and ponder. If the babies did heed the herbal brew and come, Sapphire could leave. But problems remained. How could I get the Philadelphia-bound group off before awkward rumors about Sophie started? For that matter, how would I get Sapphire to Richmond?

Horace would have to take Sapphire. Papa was the priority. I would write a full explanation of their mission, in case they were stopped, and I'd have to trust that would keep them safe en route. Horace's heavy work would fall to Ruby and her boys, though they weren't strong enough. I saw no solution to the problems Sophie posed. I said aloud, "God help me."

There was an answer to my prayer.

From the gathering dark, a familiar voice said, "Miss Evelyn? You alone?" I looked up, startled.

"Dan?" I whispered back to the shrubbery. "Is that you? Is Eli with you?"

I knew Daisy's brothers would come for her, but . . . now? With all the other problems? And this soon? I wasn't ready to see Daisy go.

"Yup. It's me'n Eli—somebody else, too," said Dan's voice with a chuckle. "Me'n Eli, we've brought Miss Sophie's Mr. Theo to marry her." From the shrubbery, three forms emerged. I might not have recognized Sapphire's sons in the dusk had I seen them first; they were in Quaker garb. As was the third man.

"Theophilus?" I questioned. Could it really be? How on earth could Theo have turned up now?

"Is Sophie all right?" he asked, and it was undoubtedly Theo. "Where's Atha? I need to thank her."

"Thank her?"

"For letting me know." Theo bounded up the steps to the porch, pulled off his hat, and squeezed me as I came to meet him. We had hardly been on such terms before, but I remembered his exuberance. He kissed me. "Coz!" he cried, and waved Dan and Eli to join us.

I was stunned. Poised somewhere between disbelief and excitement. Theo, of all people, when we needed him! And brought, apparently, by Atha—who, I knew, disapproved of him.

"By God, it's good to finally get here!" he said, opening the front door without ceremony. "Sophie! Atha!" he called, leaving me and Sapphire's sons behind.

In the lamplight of the hallway, I examined Dan and Eli. Except for darker complexions, they resembled my Philadelphia uncles and male cousins, togged out in tidy dark outfits and broad-brimmed hats.

"You look like Quakers," I said. "Are you in disguise?"

"No, Miss Evelyn. We're Friends now, sure enough," said Eli. "The Meeting's been so good to us, we figured we'd join up and be Quakers, too." He rolled his eyes at Dan and chuckled. "Not that the clothes ain't been handy, once or twice along the road to here. Do we have tales to tell!" Then he started after Theo, calling "Mammy! Mammy! Me'n Dan is here!"

The kitchen overflowed. Dan and Eli were hugging Sapphire and Daisy. "Told you we'd be back for you!" Eli shouted over the babble. Their aunts and cousins and Horace hovered, waiting their turn. Rebecca stood at the sink, turning a puzzled face from one person to the next.

Mama sat in a kitchen chair, looking dazedly at Theophilus embracing Sophie, who was crying to beat the band.

Atha was sitting on the edge of the kitchen table, near Mama, patting her shoulder and saying, "Everything's all right now," as Isabel kept repeating, "What's going *on*, Atha?" Nelly bounced up and down with the excitement of so much to tell, once she got it all sorted out. Joycelyn and little Annalee, in their nighties, peered from the landing of the back stairs, hoping not to be ordered back to bed.

Suddenly, Sophie gasped, yelped, and doubled over.

Mama gripped the table's edge, stifled a moan, and said, "He's coming, Sapphire."

Silence blanketed the room. Annalee's voice rang clear, as she said, "Joycelyn, look! Something's the matter with Mama and Sophie."

———•———

SAPPHIRE assured us "first babies take time," so Theophilus and I arranged for a wedding ceremony before Sophie's labor got worse. Isabel organized the youngsters, and they wandered the garden in the dark, plucking bouquets to decorate the parlor.

Theo showed Mama that he'd brought the proper papers; the permissions of his parents and Sophie's were in order, as well as the blessings of the elders of the Meeting, and a copy of the vows. There was an attestation, too, to be signed by witnesses. Dan and Eli and Atha, as members of the Meeting, would sign first, then others could, too.

"Is that lawful marriage in Virginia?" I asked.

"Don't matter to me," said the bridegroom-to-be. "If not, we'll just do it over again at home. Meantime, the baby will be born in wedlock as far as God and our relatives are concerned."

Atha took Sophie off to freshen her for the ceremony. I heard Atha as they headed for Olympus: "Well, Sophie, I did write Theo without thy consent, but I had to. Thee refused to break thy pledge not to write, but I'd promised Mama I'd look after thee." She took her sister's arm to help her down the steps.

———

Sophie laughed and said, "I forgive thee, Atha." The screen slammed behind them.

MAMA and Sapphire were in the birthing room by the time the parlor was ready. They'd miss the ceremony.

Daisy and Rebecca had placed flowers and candles on the mantel, and magnolia leaves in the empty fireplace. The children had changed into clothes they thought suitable for a wedding. Atha escorted a radiant Sophie to join Theo on the hearth.

The ceremony itself took less time than even these minimal preparations. Atha read the permissions and then Sophie and Theophilus married themselves, stating their vows as husband and wife.

Sophie's face glowed from within as well as from the candlelight, and Theophilus supported her so well through every vow and labor pain that I suspicioned Aunt Honor was wrong: In this instance, there was no sacrifice in marriage.

Dan and Eli signed as witnesses. I stepped forward to do the same and saw they'd signed "Daniel Jewell" and "Elijah Jewell."

"They've taken a last name," I said to Daisy, who was waiting her turn.

"Yes," said Daisy. "I'm taking *two* new names to use in Philadelphia." With a small flourish of the pen she wrote "Marguerite Jewell." She flushed and smiled, pleasantly embarrassed. "Mrs. Rawley's been calling me *Marguerite*. She says *Daisy's* too plain. The French for 'daisy' dresses it up."

"Then you're really leaving with Dan and Eli?" I whispered.

Daisy gave my hand a squeeze. "I've got to. It's my chance. It would break Mammy's heart if I backed down now. I'll miss you though, almost as much as I'll miss her."

I blinked back tears. "Oh, Daisy, how will I manage?"

Daisy smiled, though her own lashes were suspiciously damp. "Rebecca's staying, remember. You two'll do fine."

Ruby, Pearl, and Horace stepped forward to make marks beside their names, written onto the witness list by Eli.

The ceremonies were over. Isabel herded the younger children to bed, and Atha led Sophie down the hall toward the birthing room.

Ruby produced wineglasses on a silver tray, and Horace poured the wine Mama had ordered up. The few of us left to enjoy a toast drank a small glassful to hail the groom. The crystal clinked merrily, and the liquid glowed when I held my glass to the candlelight.

I was relaxed, as I hadn't been in weeks. Sophie was safely married. Three strong young men could drive the carriage to Philadelphia. Sapphire was handling the births. Tomorrow I'd decide how to get her to Richmond—and Horace home safely, after taking her.

A brief knock sounded on the front door; then booted feet strode the hallway. In the next seconds, my mind tensed for possible danger, and I relaxed again. Must be Liza.

No one else would be so informal, so she must have ridden over with news, though it was late. Liza would keep our secrets—if only Nelly could be as easily depended upon! I was already concocting half-truths to tell.

After all, there was a good deal to explain: a sudden bride, too many babies, escaped slaves in Quaker garb, White and Negro folks socializing over crystal glasses of wine. Even Liza might find this hard to handle.

Not Liza, but my cousin Dabney and young Spottswood strode over the threshold.

Never, I assure you, were visitors less welcome.

Twenty-seven

In Which Dabney
Surprises Me Again

DABNEY and I stared in mutual horror. It's odd, but I knew he also wished Spottswood to hell and gone. We hadn't the stomach to air family affairs in front of him.

Spotts, however, did not retire gracefully to permit this. As Rebecca slipped behind Ruby and edged toward the door, he grabbed her forearm. "This must be that gal you fancied, Chamberlyn," he leered. "I vow I fancy her myself."

Without looking at him, Dabney said, "She belongs to Evelyn now. She bought Rebecca from my sister. You'd best let her go." He glanced toward Rebecca, and his face softened a moment, then he turned to stare at his companion, and spoke through his teeth, *"I said, let her go, Spotts. Now."*

Spottswood shrugged and released Rebecca's arm. She vanished into the hall. Dan made a move to follow, tugging Eli. Dabney focused on them. "Lord above!" he said. "Those aren't Quakers. They're Uncle Landon's missing boys, Dan and Eli."

"Looks like a party to celebrate their homecoming," his companion drawled. "All these White folks and Niggers sharing wine by candlelight." He grinned. "Chamberlyn, seems to me you've really got to take over this place before your family's reputation is shot to hell."

He dropped the pretense of amusement, and his eyes narrowed. "First off, what're we going to do about these renegade boys?" he said, gesturing toward the Jewells.

"My uncle never chased them, and they're back. I don't reckon we have to do anything," Dabney answered, to my surprise.

"They surely don't look like they're planning to stay," said Spottswood. "Seems they think they're Quakers now." His gaze shifted to Theo. "And who in tarnation is this?"

Dabney looked at me, puzzled.

"Theophilus is my cousin Sophie's husband," I announced.

"When did Sophie marry?" Dabney asked.

"This evening. Here." I gestured toward the candles with my wineglass. "We were celebrating."

"Where's the bride?" Spottswood snickered, pretending to check each face. "She's conspicuously missing. And so is your mama, Miss Evelyn."

He moved closer and looked me full in the face.

I'd won our first fight with a swat from the riding crop. As unforgivable in a woman as a slave. The nasty smile that creased his face without changing his eyes told me he was gloating over finding me in yet another precarious situation. I didn't doubt Spotts intended to teach me a lesson and have his revenge.

"You-all holding a wedding without the bride and hostess? Or are you-all merely flouting the Fugitive Slave Law in grand style?" he drawled.

"Dabney," I said, turning to my cousin, "I need to talk with you privately." I looked around the group. "Please, everyone clear out."

"Good idea," said Theo. He set his glass on the table and moved toward the door. "Let's all do that."

"Not so fast." Spottswood ignored him and stared at me. "I'm gonna make sure these particular fugitives don't vanish." He turned to Dabney. "What your uncle *wants* makes no never-mind in this case, though they're his property. Can't let dear Miss Evelyn give these boys a head start to get away again."

"Look, Spotts," said Dabney, "this is my family and my business. Just go outside and wait with our horses, please."

Spottswood shook his head. "No," he said. "Every man is obliged under the law to catch runaway Niggers. Mebbe I can leave the rest of this-here mess to you"—he glanced around generally—"but I know my duty where slaves are concerned."

He strolled over to stare at the witness list. "Huh. Look here, Chamberlyn. Seems Niggers are witnesses now."

He turned a face of disgust on me. "Slaves can't testify in any court of law," he stated. "Ain't you ashamed to put your signature here, next to these marks? *Jewell?* My God, the dogs and cats'll be giving themselves last names next."

He scanned the group. "That's Daniel. That's Elijah. Who the hell is this Mar-*gue*-rite Jewell person?"

Daisy stepped forward. "I'm Marguerite Jewell," she stated flatly, staring in his face.

"Ah, the chit from the Nigger schoolhouse." Spottswood advanced toward her with a half-smile. "We'll take her back to Richmond, too, with those boys."

"Don't you touch her," I said, stepping in front of him.

"I'll do as I please, Miss Evelyn Chamberlyn," he answered. "The law's the law, and runaways have got to be caught and punished." He reached in his jacket and pulled out a pistol, which he pointed at Dan, not me.

Dabney moved to my side. "Spotts," he said, "you may be right about Dan and Eli, but you can't insult a young lady in her own parlor. And Daisy's not a runaway." He put a hand on my shoulder, a protective move—but one that held me back.

Something about Dabney was different, now. I wondered whether the schoolhouse incident, which had enraged Spottswood, had reformed him. Possibly he'd been genuinely ashamed. It was Spottswood who'd urged the attack on Daisy; perhaps Dabney had followed against his better judgment.

Could I keep my cousin from following again?

I looked toward Dabney. "You can't let him do this."

Spottswood gestured with the gun. "I'll shoot both them boys if I have to," he said.

I believed him. Guess Dabney did, too. He tried compromise.

"Take the boys, then, but leave Daisy." Dabney jerked his chin toward the door. "Wait by the horses. I won't be long."

"No." I pulled my shoulder away and turned to face him. "Now you listen to me, Dabney Chamberlyn. Our grandfather set Sapphire free when she was born. And the children follow the mother. So Dan and Eli and D—Marguerite, they're free, too."

"That's been the rumor," Dabney said. "Nobody ever found the papers, though." His voice went up a bit, as if his statement were a question. No doubt about it, Dabney wanted no part of Spottswood's plans this time, if he could lawfully refuse.

"I have," I stated. "You wait here." They stood as they'd been told, to my surprise.

I picked up a candle, jerked my gown up in front, and leapt up the stairs to my room. Fortunately, the document was near the top of the heap. An edge of parchment peeked from below several notebooks. I pinched it, pulled it out, and pushed the block of pigeonholes back in place.

In two minutes I was handing the manumission to Dabney.

He read, then looked up at Spottswood. "She's right. It's the old man's signature, for sure, and it's dated way back. Probably the date is Sapphire's birthday. They're free."

"Parchment like that, it's dry. Burns easy," Spottswood remarked, reaching for a candle. "Real easy."

In a move so smooth as to be invisible, Theophilus had knocked Spottswood down, rolled him over, and twisted his arms. The gun spun across the floor. "Belt, please," Theo remarked mildly to Eli, who stripped off this article and handed it over. Theo bound Spottswood's arms behind his back.

"If thee doesn't mind, Coz," he said to me, "I'll just tuck this doodad away for safekeeping." He stuffed the parchment into an inner jacket pocket. "It might be handy on the way home. I do believe we'd best be off to Philadelphia as soon as possible," he added. "Don't want this gentleman to rally reinforcements, once we take the belt off and let him run."

He rose from the prone shape of Spottswood, and nodded to Dabney. "Quakers deplore violence, you know," he said—but he grinned broadly.

"Now, everybody get out and let these two kinfolks talk like they've asked us to do. You might pocket that gun," he added to Dabney. "Give it back in Richmond."

"Put these glasses down, everybody, before we break them," Ruby said, setting her own on the central parlor table. She and Pearl led the way, followed by Daisy and her brothers, with Horace and Theo bringing up the rear, Spottswood between them.

Theo dashed back, collected the witness list. "Do you think

we could get away this very night, once the baby comes?" he asked.

I frowned a little, thinking of Mama's recoveries. "Most ladies lie abed for weeks, but Sapphire always makes Mama walk the next day," I said. "Sapphire says, 'That's one reason why ladies do poorly and fieldhands do good.' " I nodded. "She also says Sophie's healthy as a horse. Ask her, but I think she'll agree a coach ride would be safe."

"Safer, anyway, than chancing a lynching of me or her sons by that hellhound," Theo said, his face grim. Then he assumed his usual amused demeanor. "I don't think Mr. Spotts has enjoyed this evening nearly as much as we have, Coz."

He bowed to Dabney, then to me. "Have a good chat, you two." And he disappeared through the door.

I moved to shut the door before I let my temper out. "*What* are you doing here?" I spat at Dabney. "Breaking in at this time of night? With that worthless worm Spottswood?"

"I hardly broke in," he replied. "I've never stood on ceremony at the Big House. Be reasonable, Evvy. I couldn't have guessed you'd be entertaining escaped slaves and Negro folks in the parlor. I didn't bring trouble on purpose.

"Spotts and I were going to return to the troop right off, after leaving our wounded. Then Uncle Landon had a conniption when he heard Horace would be bringing Sapphire to Richmond. 'Can't take them both away at once,' he said. 'Evvy needs them.' So I volunteered to fetch Sapphire."

Dabney passed his hat from one hand to the other and paced away from me. "Evvy, your papa is pretty bad off. Really. When Spotts said he'd ride along, having company sounded cheering. I didn't figure on any problems."

He turned, and looked me in the eye. "Spotts is trouble. I see now he bears you a grudge. But he's a good soldier. Fought like a tiger. Our troop's better off for him."

"He's trash, Dabney, and you know it. Men may admire him, but he'd better expend his malice on the enemy and spare us. The Yankees can't kill him soon enough for me."

Dabney bit back the retort I expected. After a pause, he said, "If you'll find Sapphire, I'll be off. The sooner, the better. We borrowed a mule at Wright's Rest to carry her, along with any amount of cures and potions she'll need. And I'd like to pay my respects to your mama, so's I can tell Uncle she's fine."

"She's having the baby just now," I said. "So, she and Sapphire are both too busy to greet you."

He flushed, then nodded. "I'll wait till she's safe; Uncle will want to know how she and the baby are doing."

"And whether he has a son?" The sarcasm lashed out before I knew it was coming. "Or do you want to know that yourself?"

Dabney flushed again, and his mouth tightened. "Look, Evvy," he said. "I'm not proud of our last meeting. I apologize. And I didn't come to fight. I came to get help for Uncle Landon. I happen to care for him, too. And I am *not* responsible for our grandfather's Will."

"You'll take advantage of it, however."

"Wouldn't you, Evvy, if you could?"

That was too true to deny. I made a growling sound, and walked away.

Rebecca opened the door a crack, and peeped in. "Miss Evelyn, baby's about here; Sapphire said to fetch you."

Dabney jumped at the sound of her voice, and whirled to catch a glimpse as she flitted out, escaping his view.

I started back toward the door, but he put out a hand to delay me. "Cousin, what you're thinking isn't true." He had the grace to flush, but looked me in the eye, as he announced, "Believe me, I truly love Rebecca."

I stared in openmouthed astonishment. "I'm not a fool, Dabney," I managed. "Perhaps you do care about Papa, but what you feel for Rebecca isn't love. She's terrified of you."

"I know she is," he replied, his mouth drawn in what appeared to be genuine misery. He twisted the hat again, and now avoided looking at me. "I fooled myself I could win her over. Of course, we couldn't marry, but I thought I could make that right. Persuade her to love me anyway. I hated you for buying her. At first."

"And you don't now? You changed your mind?"

"Mostly." He gave a small grin. "You are one hard woman to like, Cousin Evelyn. You give me grief every time we meet."

Then he was serious again. "I spoke with Captain Montcure on the way to Richmond; I knew she'd once belonged to him. I needed to say her name. I still do. She haunts me."

I began to believe him, but I put on a skeptical face.

"Montcure said he'd made that mistake. Fell in love with a beautiful, talented slave woman. She loved him back, but 'Love ain't enough,' he said. 'We were outcasts, and miserable. If you love her, you'll leave her alone.'"

Dabney shivered visibly. "He near cried, said he was ashamed to be glad when his woman died and he thought he could start over." He paused. "But then he said, 'Even starting over's a problem. Whatever you do, or don't do, ends by hurting people you care about. Leave her alone, boy. You don't need the guilt, and she don't need the pain.'"

Dabney paced off, then back, and stood in front of me. "I do love her. I know I do, because I want what's good for her. You've done right by her. I thank you."

His voice broke, and he turned to lean one hand on the door frame. "She is the most glorious creature! I may never see her again."

"Pray God, you don't," I retorted. "Her father gave you good advice."

"Her father! Montcure's her father?" His shock immediately gave way to belief. "Oh, Lord. Of course." He walked to the nearest chair and sat down hard.

"If you'll excuse me." I stalked around him toward the hall, turned in the doorway, and looked back. He was slumped over, holding his hat between his knees.

"Cousin!" I said, and he looked up. "You're a hard man to like, but I find I do. Thank you."

Then I gathered my skirts and dashed to the kitchen.

Twenty-eight

In Which I
Resemble Great-aunt Jane
More than Ever

I'D EXPECTED a crowd, but the kitchen was empty except for Rebecca, outside the birthing room door. "Where's everybody?" I asked.

"Your mama and Miss Sophie and Sapphire are in there." She nodded toward the door. "And Atha's in Olympus, packing for herself and Sophie. Pearl and Daisy are collecting for a medicine chest, so's the right aftercare fixings for Sophie will be aboard. Ruby's in the quarters packing Daisy's things."

"And the men?"

"They're in the barn, redding up the coach. Mr. Theo is bound they'll be off, soon as the baby gets here." A small frown signaled Rebecca's concern. "Will Miss Sophie be safe?"

"The coach is well sprung, the seats as comfortable as daybeds. And Daisy's experienced in aftercare." I smiled encouragement. "Sophie should do fine."

I touched her shoulder. "Rebecca, I don't want to nag—but I've filled out your papers; you can be on this coach tonight."

Rebecca shook her head. "No. I'm needed here, and Daisy and Atha can handle the journey fine." Her brow knit with worry. "You won't insist? Sapphire needs me, with Daisy gone. It's like having real family."

An infant wail filled the air, and I rushed to the birthing room door. When I glanced back, Rebecca waved me on. "Go in. I'll keep watch."

Sapphire was beside Sophie; she turned and smiled broadly. "Fine little man here. Good lungs."

"Sophie's all right?" I asked. "And Mama?"

"Both fine, Honey. I gave them my sleepy stuff that keeps them drowsy betwixt the pains. They're not real bright just now, but everything's going real nice." Sapphire put the baby on a nest of fabric, and began wiping him down.

"I thought Mama would be first."

"Thought so myself, Honey. But you never know. Miss Sophie, she pushed right on." She pulled the edges of the nest around the little creature, making a bundle. "Your mama, she drifted and slowed a bit. Just as well, to say the truth. Lets me deal with one at a time."

She placed the bundle next to the sleeping Sophie, and I tiptoed over to take a look. "He looks like Annalee and Beatrice did," I said. "I guess I thought boys would look different."

Sapphire chuckled. "Not to begin with, except down below." She shook Mama gently. "Time to work again, Miss Felicity. Don't sleep too hard."

Mama stirred, put a hand on her stomach, and mumbled. Sapphire pulled down the sheet that covered her and pushed her knees up. "That's a girl," she murmured, "I see that little head coming. About to catch me a baby here. Now push, hard, Honey. You can do it."

Mama's eyes opened; her face awoke. "Sapphire, how'm I doing?"

"Wonderful, Honey. 'Nother push now."

I'd feared the experience, but neither Mama nor Sapphire seemed distraught. There was a rhythm to their work that was nearly dancelike. Sapphire led, but Mama knew the steps as well as she did. There was a lull.

Mama sighed, and closed her eyes again.

The door opened, and Rebecca spoke. "The coach has pulled up outside the kitchen. Can I let the men in?"

Sapphire walked to the door. "Those boys stay in the yard. Men are unlucky at birthing time. You go keep 'em busy with stowing Miss Atha's trunk and the other bundles. Tell Daisy not to put the medicine on till I check the supplies."

She returned to Mama, shook her again. "Time to work, Honey. This time'll do it."

And it did. The head emerged, then Sapphire somehow turned the little figure, and the body came slickly onto the wad of material protecting the cot. Sapphire blocked the view, as she used the knife, then disposed of something into a bucket on the floor. She turned, showed the child, rubbed its feet. It cried.

"Another girl?"

She nodded as she wiped the tiny figure down, then nestled it into the waiting cloths.

"Mama wanted a boy," I said, my heart sinking. I walked over and stared at her. She'd lapsed into slumber again.

"Your mama'll love whatever she has, you know that," said Sapphire. She gave me a squeeze, then turned back to Sophie and checked her. She went to Mama and began to knead her stomach. "Gotta be sure everything's out," she said.

"Here." She motioned with her head. "You come do this a bit, while I check that medicine chest." She saw my hesitation. "Don't you worry. They'll snooze unless they're roused up. Just put your hands here, and roll gently, like this."

She smiled. "I haven't seen my boys in months, and they're leaving again," she reminded me.

I nodded. "Of course." I began to move my hands as ordered, as she hastened out the door. I took a good look at my newborn sister. For all I could see, she looked just like Sophie's child.

The minutes ticked by as I tried to make sense of the evening's events and rhythmically pressed on Mama's abdomen. Once I got the hang of it, there was nothing to do but think. My thoughts were not pleasant.

Papa was indeed very sick. I believed Dabney's claim that he'd rather have Papa live than inherit now, but he'd certainly own Chamberlyn Hall someday, and, perhaps, all too soon.

Sapphire predicted Mama would revive, given time. But what if Papa died? He'd never seemed as strong to me since his bout with mumps, and now he was seriously wounded. Could Mama survive a second loss?

Mama loved her girls, but she'd set her heart on a boy. A girl would upset her. There'd be no more babies. . . . Now, or later, the school would close, the plantation would be gone.

I could, I'd proved it, run a girls' school. I could support my sisters, even if Papa and Mama both somehow failed. *I could do it—but only if we kept the property.* Dabney was waiting outside to hear about Mama's baby.

For the third time, I felt that red rage flame—not directed at Dabney, or Papa, or even old Justin or the despicable Reverend— just fury at the injustice of being a woman. *Not fair!* I thought. *Not fair! Not, not, not!*

A cold, clear answer cut through the anger. Perhaps not

Inner Light, but certainly akin to it in the way my mind and heart and even, oddly, my *stomach* were certain-sure.

This was my chance.

I could spend my life regretting Win, leaning on Papa, begging from Dabney or Uncle Carter if Papa died, raising Isabel's children or, at best, living in Uncle Paul's house, teaching in his school. In Philadelphia, far from home.

Always, always, some man to tell me what to do.

And my students, they would go home to be stuck into stays and edifices, to be forbidden French novels and skinny-dipping. Their fathers and then their husbands would command them. Who would give them the tools to free themselves if I did not?

I looked at the sleeping women and babies, and I scooped up Sophie's son. I raced to the front yard and dashed up to Dabney. "A boy!" I said, "and Mama's fine!" I unrolled the blankets and displayed the baby's nether parts, then rolled him up again. "Sapphire'll be out soon," I added and fled indoors. I had not exactly lied, in words.

I peered through the window at the dimly lit scene outside, as I jiggled the infant in my arms. Sapphire was concentrated on her sons, huddled away from the bustle. She never mixed men with birthing, and her sons were full of their own stories. I'd wager she'd said nothing about the babies. Only she and I knew.

Sapphire would never, ever agree, but she will back me afterward, I thought. *She'll have to know before she leaves, but not till Sophie and my sister are well out of reach.* I glanced at the infant in my arms. The blankets had to be switched.

I turned from the window and unrolled both babies, the boy from a gray cloth, the girl from a yellow with blue stripes. I reversed them, tucking each next to the wrong mother. Even Sapphire would never see any difference in the tiny, half-hidden faces. Sophie and Mama slumbered peacefully on. I resumed my kneading.

WITHIN the quarter hour, Theo carried a half-sleeping Sophie to the carriage, where Atha settled her across the forward seat, tucking a pillow under her head and an afghan over her. I followed with the baby and handed her to Daisy. Atha leaned out the window. "Have Pearl alter our dresses for you and Isabel. I left most of our books."

Theo jumped in, slammed the door, and Eli swatted the horses with a loud "giddup!" Dan waved, and the dust rose behind them.

Sapphire and I waved back. She gave a long, deep sigh. "I hate to see my boys go right off again," she said, "but it's safest. Leaving now, they get a good head start on that Spottswood, long as he's stuck waiting with Marse Dabney." She gave a small sob. "And my own baby girl, gone, too."

I began to cry myself. For a moment we clung to each other.

"Excuse me, Honey," she added, pressing her kerchief to her eyes. "Would you just carry that case by the birthing room door out front to the mule?"

I was only too glad to keep busy. Sapphire checked her supplies, bundled some clothes, and directed the packing of the mule. A half hour later, she mounted the laden animal with Horace's help.

Dabney and the sullen Spottswood watched, more restive than their horses. I ran to the far side of the mule to say good-bye, and, as Sapphire leaned to kiss me, I whispered, "Mama had the boy. Sophie had the girl."

She drew back, startled. "What're you saying, Honey?"

"Did you tell your sons who had what? Because I switched

them. I put the boy by Mama, and the girl's already gone in the coach with Sophie."

She was wide-eyed, speechless. Slowly she shook her head. "My boys—they didn't ask. We had so much to talk about."

Relief flowed over me. In a spurt, the words I'd rehearsed came out. "Papa's dying. Maybe you can save him, but what if not?" I whispered. I tugged at her till she leaned down again. "What if we get turned out? What if Mama doesn't perk up?"

"You do beat all."

Dabney called out, "Evvy, quit your good-byes! We should move on—sooner we get there, the better."

"Don't tell on me, Sapphire," I begged. "What's done is done. It's on my conscience, not yours."

She shook her head, as if to clear her mind. Then she shook it again, decisively. "I ain't gonna tell, Honey. Can't change things now. Your mama and Sophie'll each be in love with the child she's got, long before I could tell them."

She sat up in the saddle and frowned down on me.

"You resemble your great-aunt Jane awful much, Child." This time she did not laugh as she said that.

In Which I
Celebrate a
Most Unusual Birthday

WHEN I woke on the morning of my eighteenth birthday, I knew nobody else would remember it. Isabel had turned thirteen in the week after Beatrice's funeral, and we hadn't celebrated that, or any others, until little Landon's recent third birthday.

Somehow, Ruby and Pearl had baked him a tiny real cake, with icing. Lannie had never seen such—his face reflected greedy bliss. Mama gave him a wrapped-string ball in a little box. Lannie loved the box more than the ball. "Birfday!" he said, sticking the ball in and out again.

I neatened the bedclothes. We tidied our own rooms these days. And celebrations were now only for babies. I thought of little Pauline in Philadelphia. How had she celebrated the day? Mail from the North had become too expensive for the rare letter to cover such trivial matters.

I pulled Atha's gown from the peg and slipped it over my head. I still missed her sorely. *How many people I've lost, since that long-ago birthday,* I thought. The past three years were filled with losses: Beatrice and Papa to death; my cousins, Daisy, Rebecca, and Sapphire to Philadelphia. Cousin Dabney had died at the Battle of Fredericksburg. I would not have expected to mourn Dabney, but I found I did.

Julius had, finally, come through on the Railroad. Once he returned, he and Sapphire decided to join their children. Rebecca's hunger for family was strong. I persuaded her to go, while she had a protective escort.

Nobody could fill the gaps left by Daisy, Rebecca, and, most of all, by Sapphire. Soon, however, women set adrift by war and widowhood turned up begging to join my staff. As more girls arrived, more help did, too.

But none of this had come easy, and the effort showed.

Liza's right, I thought as I buttoned my bodice, *I look years older.* At eighteen, I seemed at least twenty-five, and some of the time I felt nearer forty. My fourteenth birthday and the rose silk seemed a million years ago.

I styled my hair as Rebecca had taught me, and the Edifice sprang to mind. I laughed a little, over the stormy girl who'd vowed she'd grow up to do "all a man could do, and still be a true woman." *Sapphire always warned me to be careful what I wished for; I might get it.*

From my window I spotted my next two sisters heading back from the girls' dormitory to eat breakfast. Poor Isabel. Her pale prettiness faded in the Quaker clothes that suited me. That blue silk gown she'd expected was impossible. Not even homespun was available. Leastways, not for Confederate money. Rumor was, anything could be had from the blockade runners for cash or Union dollars.

And Nelly, at fourteen, was resentful. To her, the war was a personal affront, as was almost any other event. "It's not fair!" was her constant cry.

I went down the hall, missing the long-gone smell of bacon

for breakfast. The old nursery's door was open; a glance proved my two youngest sisters were up and out. They, at least, were little trouble.

Annalee barely remembered Papa or prewar delights. She continued to put Isabel to the blush by blurting truths, but secretly I found that endearing.

Of them all, only Joycelyn, now nearing twelve, shared my feelings of release. She had a sense of humor I could only envy. My old horror story of the Reverend turned comic in her retelling, and she wasn't above entertaining her classmates by faking fainting fits induced, she said, by Latin.

Joycelyn's nonsense soothed me—it confirmed my Cause as worthy. How could I be content with evil things? That Papa could never return to change Olympus back into Chamberlyn Academy? That I'd usurped Dabney's inheritance? That I'd injured Mama and Sophie? Only my conviction that other girls, innocent girls, benefited from my sins eased my conscience.

I told myself *Jane would understand*, as I descended the stairs. *What*, I wondered, *will happen when this interminable war does end?* Even now, parents bartered for students' keep, sending wagons of foodstuffs. *Will they pay once the boys come home?*

Most older girls yearned for prewar comforts and eager beaux. I knew for harsh fact that our meager stores were better than most. And men were scarce.

Younger girls relished school. One of my fondest moments came when a girl announced: "I used to want to be a boy, because boys were *allowed*, and we weren't. But here we do anything they do but fight. So, I wouldn't switch." My Inner Light had danced.

I wistfully recalled birthdays of the past as I took a square of corn bread and a boiled egg from the sideboard.

Mama had eaten, but remained to chat and watch Lannie explore. After Papa's death, she'd pulled herself together to nurture the new infant and comfort the rest of us, but she remained passive. Her mischievous side—the part I'd especially loved—was gone forever.

Oh, Lord, I prayed, as I often did when I saw Lannie, *please let Pauline be as satisfactory a child. For Sophie's sake.* But I knew He wasn't fooled; I petitioned for my own conscience.

Nelly pushed her corn bread around, while Isabel ate grits.

"No jam, even?" said Nelly.

"I'm saving the last jar," Mama said. "You might find some honey in the pantry."

Nelly subsided. She didn't like to wait on herself. Isabel walked out, returning with honey. Nelly muttered an ungracious thanks.

To my relieved delight, Liza tapped on the window, then let herself in. She'd ridden over with mail, that now-rare treat.

"Win came through last night, on military dispatch from Richmond to Fredericksburg, and brought this from your uncle Carter." She handed a mail pouch to Mama and proceeded, uninvited, to fill a plate. "He couldn't stay." She gave me a reproachful glance, and waited for my sisters to support her.

"If a *certain person* had treated Win better, we'd see more of him," Nelly said, with an angry toss of her curls.

Isabel only pinched her lips in disapproval.

Liza smiled at my irritation, then changed the subject. "My mama rises so late, I don't make breakfast nowadays. My, but Pearl's corn bread is good." She made a comic face. "My cooking is awful beyond awful. And honey! Lord a'mighty, what a treat!" She filled a bowl with grits, dolloped honey over. She sighed with pleasure. "I do fancy breakfast, you know."

Mama looked up, face alight. "This letter's from Daisy. Honor surely paid a fortune for delivery, but the news is fine, though several months old. Guess what? Sophie and Theo are expecting. The Jewells are together in a rental house, but Daisy's still teaching at Honor and Paul's. Their Meeting is planning a school for Negro girls, and Marguerite Jewell will be headmistress."

"Wonderful! And what about Rebecca?" I asked.

"She's apprenticed to a milliner, and doing well."

Isabel nodded. "She's talented at hat trimming."

Mama folded the first letter, and slit a second. "An embarrassment of riches, today," she gloated. "This is from Carter, only a few weeks old. He must have been holding both of these to send by Win." She held the letter farther away to read. "Why—heavens!" she said. "Rebecca has become an heiress!"

"That's impossible!" said Nelly. "How could she inherit? She was a *slave*. She didn't *have* relatives."

I ignored her. "How does Uncle Carter know?"

"His friend Mr. Montcure came to Carter with a letter, written by a cousin settling a family estate. The cousin needed to find a girl named Rebecca."

She looked up, and smiled. "It seems the cousin's mother had been secretly investing money old Adelaide Montcure regularly sent for this girl. She even expected to give the girl a home, when Rebecca was old enough to send North."

Mama glanced down. "The cousin figured Mr. Montcure might know how to find her. And, of course, he did."

A thought occurred. *If Mr. Montcure and this executor were cousins, then*—I spoke softly, looking at Liza. "The two old ladies were sisters."

Liza's eyes widened in agreement. The mystery of Rebecca's

trunk was solved. "The clothes were for Rebecca's trip North, but she couldn't bear to let her darling go—then it was too late," Liza ventured, low enough to avoid notice.

"How much money did she get?" Nelly demanded to know, even as Liza spoke. Isabel coughed with mortification, as Mama gave a reproving glance. "Carter says merely 'a tidy sum.' "

Liza, who'd been eating while listening, now spoke up. "Miss Felicity, there's a package, too; don't neglect that."

Mama pulled a small box, tied with string, from the pouch. Lannie trotted over and reached for the parcel. "No, Sweetie, not for you," Mama said. She turned to me in surprise. "It's yours, Evvy. It's Carter's hand, dated later than his letter."

She passed me the box, then pulled Lannie onto her lap. "Let's watch Evvy open it," she said.

I fumbled with the string, and Liza reached to cut it with a knife. "Hurry up," she begged.

A note fell from the wrappings. Uncle Carter's scrawl announced: "Rebecca sent ample funds for this. Virginia's thrilled to have solid money for a trousseau, now she's engaged."

I opened the lid, and removed a tissue-wrapped object. Suddenly, I knew what it was.

Yes, there among the paper gleamed the locket.

"Oh, my!" gasped Isabel.

"Not fair!" said Nelly.

"Birfday!" crowed little Landon.

"God A'mighty, it *is* your birthday, isn't it!" said Liza. "I'd forgot."

Mama pulled the locket from the tissue. She stood to clasp the chain around my neck. "If only Papa could do this," she whispered. "My good and lovely daughter, where would we be without you?"

Good? If she only knew.

I popped the locket open and stared at Great-aunt Jane. I could swear her image winked at me—but perhaps it was the tears that brought that illusion.

As Sapphire had said, long ago. "There's times when you just got to do what you got to do, even if it's wrong."

Inner Light from one side of my family, and Brimstone from the other. I couldn't regret either.

Sapphire was right, as she usually is. Everybody gets born for a reason.

Afterword

EVERY person and incident in this book is fictional, but I've relied heavily on research about the period.

Some episodes reflect my own family's oral history. (My grandmother saw her little brother go up in flames and later attended a Ball with the mumps. Her family album also displayed a photograph of a little dead sister, fascinating me as a child.) Other events are based on private written records left by women and girls during the Civil War (including the scrapbook kept by my great-great-aunt Belle during and after the war), as well as words of men in sermons, articles, and newspapers.

As I planned this book, I discovered a widespread belief that nothing changed for Southern women after the Civil War. A quarter of adult Southern men died during the war. Women had to change, and they did. Why, then, this lack of credit?

Countless articles and books discuss Seneca Falls, where Northerners began a well-documented fight for women's rights, focused on the vote. Our modern fixation on suffrage is partly responsible for the view that Southerners "did nothing."

A second reason lies in worshipful records honoring the Lost Cause, face-saving efforts designed to reassure defeated, deeply damaged men. Writers portrayed women, children, and former slaves as thrilled by the return of their "protectors." Recent depictions of slavery have corrected the myth of the Eternally Devoted Slave, and rightly so. The myth of the Belle, however, lingers on.

Truth to tell, affection did exist between patriarchal husband

and wife, or master and slave. But resentment existed, too. Early historians chose to preserve the former; recent ones often emphasize the latter. Neither is the full story.

By the war's end, women raised to dependency had years of experience in coping with intolerable conditions. The Belle became enterprising. Otherwise, her family starved in rags in shabby quarters.

These women now knew that men, marriage, government, and even religion could fail. The vote must have seemed irrelevant. Safety for themselves and their daughters had to be within themselves; they faced an uncertain future. Education and jobs were their answers.

Working with young girls was one respectable route toward economic independence, and provided the bonus of new opportunities for the next generation. Women founded academically challenging schools and colleges, athletic programs, summer camps, and scouting activities: confidence-builders for women and girls alike.

Whatever their accomplishments, however, their self-esteem demanded that they seem dependent ladies, not independent women. In portraits and photographs they appear fragile. They tend to have white hair softly piled around a sweet face, set off by lace collars. This facade fooled no one who actually knew them. My parents called them "iron hands in velvet gloves"; a more recent term is "steel magnolias."

Nevertheless, common courtesy demanded that gentlemen should not expose women's competence to the world. Fortunately—and in large part due to them—our history is no longer written only by gentlemen. I think it is time someone "told on" these women.

I hope Evvy does them justice.

Sources

Annals of America, The: A House Dividing: 1850–1857. Vol. 8. New York: Encyclopedia Britannica, Inc., 1968.

The Crisis of the Union: 1858–1865. Vol. 9. New York: Encyclopedia Britannica, Inc., 1968.

Chang, Ina. *A Separate Battle: Women and the Civil War.* New York: Puffin Books, 1991.

Clinton, Catherine. *The Other Civil War: American Women in the Nineteenth Century.* New York: Hill and Wang, 1984.

Ehrenreich, Barbara, and Deirdre English. *For Her Own Good: 150 Years of the Experts' Advice to Women.* Garden City, N.Y.: Anchor Books, 1979.

*Faust, Drew Gilpin. *Mothers of Invention: Women of the Slaveholding South in the American Civil War.* Chapel Hill, N.C.: University of North Carolina Press, 1994.

Green, Harvey. *The Light of the Home: An Intimate View of the Lives of Women in Victorian America.* New York: Pantheon Books, 1983.

*Horowitz, Helen Lefkowitz. *The Power and Passion of M. Carey Thomas.* New York: Alfred A. Knopf, 1994.

*Klaus, Susan L., and Mary Porter Martin. *A Part of Us Forever: A Centennial History of St. Catherine's School, 1890–1990.* Richmond, Va.: 1989.

Plante, Ellen M. *Women at Home in Victorian America: A Social History.* New York: Facts on File, 1997.

*Woodward, C. Vann, and Elisabeth Muhlenfeld. *The Private Mary Chesnut: The Unpublished Civil War Diaries.* New York: Oxford University Press, 1984.

Sources marked with * contain original material